CHRISTMAS
Wishes
an irish tradition

CHRISTMAS
Wishes

an irish tradition
BOOK THREE

J.L. LAWRENCE

JLL PUBLISHING

Christmas Wishes is a work of fiction.
Names, characters, places, and incidents are the products of the author's imagination or are used fictitiously. Any resemblance to actual events, locales, or persons, living or dead, is entirely coincidental.

Cover and Interior Design by Kenny Halcomb.
Edited by Jeanne Hardt

CHRISTMAS
Wishes
an irish tradition

Chapter One

"Here's to the last year of our decree." Annie grinned. "And our thirty-first birthday. We're getting old." She leaned back and wiped a hand across her brow as if in relief. "No man in sight for me."

"Don't think you're getting off so easy, Sis." Gabby smirked. "This is your year to find true love. I don't think you'll escape fate."

Mark rolled his eyes. "No offense, but all this love stuff is a little girly. Let's talk about my boy, Nate, instead." Both girls punched him—one on each shoulder.

"*Ouch.* Was talking about kids a little girly, too?" He groaned. "What have you all done to me?"

Laughter filled the small Italian restaurant in their hometown of Three Forks, Montana. Annie loved the town and her home, and her siblings had created their homes there, too. Yet, she yearned for so much more. She wanted adventure and to explore all the wonders of the world. Now that her siblings had found their perfect mates and had started families of their own, she'd have to do all her traveling alone. It hurt more than she cared to admit. Life wasn't the same without the dynamic trio.

A sadness crept over Annie as she watched her sister and brother bicker about a scene in one of Mark's new mystery science-fiction novels. He'd taken their advice and created an alien detective who traveled to multiple dimensions to deliver justice to the galaxies. Gabby created the covers and had won awards, and his books had become bestsellers. They did it all from their homes in Montana. With Ally and Jake by their sides, they'd carved out a perfect life for themselves, but where did that leave *her*?

"Since you mentioned him, how is Nate doing?" Annie tried to redirect her thoughts and focus on her adorable nephew.

"You saw him yesterday," Mark dryly remarked. "He hasn't changed much in twenty-four hours."

Annie swatted at him. "I mean overall, butthead. You and Ally had such a quick wedding. Not sure why you got married just *before* Valentine's Day. You could have waited a few days and had an actual Valentine's Day wedding. That would've been romantic."

"It was romantic." Mark jiggled his brows.

"And it only came together that fast thanks to your wonderful sisters," Gabby interjected.

"Very true." Annie nodded. "Then, the two of you adopted Nate and jumped head first into the whole family thing—not to mention all your new book releases. Be honest, how is everything? It's hard for me to snoop since I live full-time at Moonbeam."

"Yet, it's like you're *always* there," Mark quipped and tugged Annie's hair. "It's great. Truly. Sadie has been a blessing and a big part of Nate's life. She's written down all sorts of stories about his biological parents, so we can continue to tell him about his first parents for years to come. Nate fit perfectly into our lives.

"Ally has added a new partner to the vet clinic, so she has more time at home. I work from there as well, and it allows me to travel when I need to for my books. I can't explain it, but everything fell perfectly into place. Easy as breathing."

"I sense something else in your story, Bro," Annie needled him. "You're hiding something."

"I assumed you two would figure it out, so I asked Ally if I could share some news with you." Mark paused with a mischievous grin.

"Well, what is it?" Gabby demanded. "Don't keep us in suspense."

"Ally is pregnant." Mark winced when both Gabby and Annie squealed in delight.

Annie nearly tackled him as she wrapped her arms around him. "I'm so happy for both of you." Gabby copied her sentiment, and the two of them nearly smothered their brother.

Annie was happy. Wasn't she?

It stung a bit that her two siblings immediately launched into a conversation about babies, and she couldn't be a part of it. Two years had passed since Gabby made a Duncan triplet decree that each sibling would find their true love. Time had almost run out, and Annie still didn't see any signs of a perfect mate headed in her direction, and she knew every male in Three Forks. That knowledge had led her to accept a new opportunity.

"Since we're sharing," she boldly said, "I just found out that the Dublin art gallery I told you about has chosen my art pieces to exhibit for their Christmas Gala this year. It's a huge honor. They plan to feature all the Irish landscapes that I've been working on the past several months, and—"

Mark wrapped her in a big bear hug, cutting off her words. Gabby grabbed her from the other side. They probably looked ridiculous to everyone else in the restaurant.

"We're so proud of you!" Gabby kissed the side of Annie's head, then sat back in her seat. "When's the event?"

"That's the tricky part." Annie hesitated. Her stomach churned as she thought about their reactions. "The event is on Christmas Eve. It's a charity thing, and I can't say no. They want me to be there in person for the gala."

Gabby's swift intake of breath increased Annie's anxiety, but she had to finish her explanation. "I won't be home until the day after Christmas."

"But we've never been apart for Christmas. *Ever,*" Gabby protested. "Not since our birth. This is big."

"Calm down, Sis." Mark placed his hand over Gabby's and gave her a warning look. "Annie has worked hard for this honor, and we need to support her. We can celebrate Christmas when she returns. The date on the calendar doesn't matter as long as we're together for the holiday."

"It's not the same, but I understand," Gabby relented. "It's your time to shine without us standing behind you. Maybe we can come see the exhibit and fly back together."

"Absolutely not!" Annie insisted. "The two of you will not leave your families at Christmas. Gabby, you have three babies that need their mother. And Mark, you and Ally have Nate and a new addition to prepare for. It's just for one year. I won't have you separated from your children. I can't bear that."

"Annie, you're right," Mark consoled her. "We'll celebrate a day or two later this year. The kids don't know what day it is anyway. No big deal. Gabby?"

"Of course, we'll celebrate when you get back home." Gabby cleared her throat, and Annie knew her sister fought hard to control her emotions and hide the tears. "In fact, I'll save the gifts, and we'll open them just like Christmas morning."

"I do have one small change to your plan if that's okay." Mark met Annie's eyes. "Gabby and I will come see the show on Christmas Eve. I've made some good friends over the years, and some of them have private jets. I've never seen the need for such extravagance until now. I'll call in a favor, and we'll have the best of both worlds."

"No, Mark, I just can't—"

"We'll stand with you as we always have," Mark interrupted again, then smiled and wiped the tear that had escaped down her cheek.

"You bet we will." Gabby took her other hand. "And it'll give Jake a little bonding time with the three kiddos. He'll appreciate me more than ever when we return. We're the Duncan triplets. Give us the details, and we'll be there."

Annie swiped at the moisture continuing to escape down her cheeks. "You two are the best ever." She grasped their hands. "I'm lucky and thankful to have you both in my life."

"I *am* pretty great." Mark preened, then grunted as Annie softly kicked him under the table.

Gabby raised her glass. "To our Duncan triplet decree and the incredible bond we share. May we continue to let love and light guide us through life. One by one, we each will fall. Our true loves shall all be revealed. May each of us be guided to find our happily ever after."

"To the Duncan triplet decree." Annie and Mark raised their glasses to meet hers.

As the glasses met, a spark ran down the length of Annie's arm. She hadn't felt that kind of jolt since that long ago day, when they stood in front of the wishing well.

An alarming thought coursed through her mind. What if her true love wasn't a person but her art? Maybe she wasn't meant for a traditional *happy ever after* like Gabby and Mark.

Annie tapped her fingers while she waited for Gabby to answer the phone. Her interfering sister had stepped over the line this time. Gabby's obsession with the wishing well had to be dealt with.

"You better be on death's doorstep for waking

me up at this hour," Gabby grumbled. "You realize I have three babies that don't believe in long sleeps."

"Why didn't you tell me about this last night? How did you know?" Annie demanded.

"Girl, what the crap are you talking about?" Gabby's grogginess began to fade.

"I woke up to someone knocking on my door. I opened it, and there was a package addressed to me." Annie paused, expecting her sister to fess up. "Well?"

"Well, what? Am I the mailman now?" Gabby huffed. "Give me a minute. I'm coming over."

Annie paced while her scheming sister made her way to Annie's cabin located just a short distance away from her on the ranch. She wrenched open the door before Gabby could knock. Her sister hadn't bothered to change out of her pajamas so that didn't bode well for her current mood.

"Why the devil have you woken me up, and why are you accusing me of sending a package I know nothing about?" Gabby grabbed Annie's coffee with one hand and placed her other hand on her hip. She downed the coffee in a few gulps. "Jessica woke up in the middle of the night which in turn woke up Izzy and Bradley. This equates to very little sleep for me, so spit it out if you have something to say."

Annie took back her coffee mug and shoved the package at her irate sister. "Here. Explain this. It has a plane ticket to Ireland that leaves today. It also includes a cottage rental in County Clare in a town called Fanore. The pictures are stunning, and it's already been paid. What kind of joke is this?"

"Annie, I don't think this is a joke." Gabby carefully studied the contents. "I didn't do this. I swear it. But it arrived the day after our birthday dinner. Just like my locket and Mark's baby, Nate. Maybe this is the sign you're supposed to follow."

"Don't be ridiculous." Annie sighed. "This is leading me halfway around the world. All joking aside, you know all that wish stuff is just coincidence."

"I'm not the one in denial." Gabby shrugged. "Last night you talked all the way home about a new series you wanted to paint, highlighting Christmas traditions in Ireland. This would give you the chance to explore and see if inspiration strikes. That packet didn't happen to include a guide, did it?"

"No, but I'm sure I can find someone to show me around and tell me about an Irish Christmas," Annie reasoned.

Gabby's eyebrows creased as she stared at her phone. "I just pulled up some information, and this doesn't appear to be a very touristy destination. Looks more like an average small town. We don't know where the package came from, and you still need to be cautious. I wish I could go with you."

"Wouldn't that be quite a sight with us pushing three babies around." Annie snapped her fingers. "I think I've got it! Sandy told me that she'd handle my arrangements for the Christmas Gala in Ireland. I briefly mentioned my new project idea. She's traveling the next couple of weeks and probably wanted me to go ahead and get settled."

"That makes sense."

Annie tried to call her manager, but she didn't

answer. "I'll send Sandy a quick email, but I'm sure that's it. Like you said, it makes sense. I'm sorry I woke you up."

"I'll miss you," Gabby whispered and her eyes moistened. "The town festivities won't be the same without you."

Annie wrapped her arm around her sister and really looked at her. They were almost identical with reddish brown hair and their soft blue eyes that always betrayed their emotions. The biggest difference in Gabby's eyes were how tired they looked all the time from adjusting to life as a new mom with triplets. Annie dreaded traveling without Gabby by her side, but she had to convince her sister that everything would be okay.

"I'll be back before you know it," Annie tried to console her. "We'll have the best Christmas celebration ever when I get back."

"Fine." Gabby sniffled. "I can't leave the house because Jake will be out working on the ranch today, and Elsie is traveling with Mick. I'll call Mark to take you to the airport while you pack. You better call me at least once a day so that I know you're safe."

"Yes, Mom. I promise." Annie smiled when Gabby narrowed her eyes.

Gabby left her to pack, and Annie hurriedly got all her things together.

About an hour passed, and Mark arrived.

Memories of past events rushed in, along with how she always depended on them to make it through a show. Maybe they did have a point, and their concern shouldn't bother her so much.

Her anger faded. She needed to do this trip to prove to herself that she could build a life of adventure all on her own just as they had. She didn't resent their happiness, but it did bring her loneliness at times.

Maybe this trip will change that...

Her suitcase weighed a ton, but she didn't want to carry two of them. Mark grunted as he hoisted it into the back of his truck. "Good thing I told you I'd mail some of your painting supplies that were too hard to pack. You never would've fit them in here—or been able to carry it if you managed to squeeze them in."

She cast a sheepish grin and slid inside the cab of his truck before she could change her mind.

Mark didn't speak for most of the drive, but Annie could tell he had something on his mind. He finally glanced at her. "Annie, are you sure about this? If something happens, we won't be there."

"Having a child has made you a worrywart." Annie smirked then laid a hand on his shoulder. "I'll be fine. This is good for me. What if my true love is simply my art? That inspiration that makes my life better? It could be my destined path."

"That's not true, Annie." Mark narrowed his eyes. "Your art is what you hide behind to prevent finding love. I've watched you use it as a shield for years. I hope this trip helps you see the difference. It's my sincerest wish for you."

She thought about his words the rest of the way

to the airport and during most of the flight. Was he right? Had she created walls around her heart? She had so easily seen the connection between Gabby and Jake, and she felt the love between Ally and Mark. What if she'd blocked her own path and prevented her wish from coming true?

She closed her eyes.

I promise myself that I will figure this out and stay open to new opportunities.

"It's never going to end, is it?" Sean O'Brien threw down the dish towel and stomped toward the kitchen.

"I'm afraid not, cousin." Cara looked at him with eyes full of sympathy. "You're thirty-five years old and not married. Nana believes you need a wife and children. That's the way she is. Ever since you came back to help your da with the pub, it's been her primary goal. She's done everything except hold public interviews. I've avoided her clutches by attending universities in America and London, yet I'm right here beside you."

He groaned. "What am I going to do? Dad won't be able to work full time again until after the new year. You're already making plans for another degree. I see it in your eyes. It's been nine months since I moved back to Ireland. I'm ready to return to my normal and peaceful life."

"You're half Irish." Cara laughed. "There'll be no peace for you."

"Not helping." Sean turned to straighten up the counter and collect dishes. They'd had a strong lunch rush today.

The first month or two at the pub had been great. After a while, he yearned for his actual job as a financial manager. Luckily, he could work from anywhere and hadn't lost many clients due to the move.

"What you need is a distraction." Cara grabbed the dishes from him and caught his eye.

"What do you mean?" Sean angled his head toward her. Cara had been the one family member to understand his predicament since she wasn't ready to be tied down, either. She always came up with a new subject to study if anyone mentioned her finding a mate. All the rest of their cousins were married with a bunch of kids. He wanted to travel and see the world—not be tied down. He'd built his financial empire and sacrificed a lot. Now, he earned the right to be frivolous. He intended to do just that as soon as his dad returned.

"Find a pretty girl and date her for a month or two. It'll help you get through the holiday season unscathed." Cara bumped him. "Am I brilliant or what?"

He grimaced and rubbed a hand over his face. "Where am I going to find a girl like that around here? They all hear wedding bells if I walk within ten feet of them."

"That's the bleeding tricky part." Cara smothered a laugh as his blind date for the night walked through the door. "But I don't think it'll be her. She has *marry me now* written all over her. Good luck with that."

Cara continued to laugh as she escaped into the kitchen. His cousin wasn't wrong. The lady coming toward him wore a tight dress, expensive perfume, manicured nails, and had perfectly styled hair. Her eyes lit up when they met his.

He inwardly groaned and braced for yet another miserable night. There had to be a limit on one person's misery, and surely, he was approaching that threshold.

The woman sauntered over with her toothy grin and seductive eyes. She held out her hand. "I'm Sally. Pleasure to meet you."

"Sean." He kept his tone brisk, not wanting to give false hope. He shook her hand.

"Where will we be eating this evening?" She smiled and advanced as if wanting to rub against him.

He stepped back and tried to hide his annoyance. "A nice little place next door." *So, I can have a quick escape.*

She seemed somewhat disappointed but followed him to the door. He opened it, and they walked the short distance to the restaurant.

"I love to travel and always stay in the best hotels." From the moment they sat down, Sally dominated the conversation. "My girls and I spend almost every weekend at a new spa or shopping excursion. I've seen so many places, including *wedding* venues. My mother has already reserved a few just in case. She's so obsessed over it." She batted her eyes.

She droned on until Sean wanted to take a running leap off the Cliffs of Moher. He'd still hear her nasally voice on the way down. All she'd talked about was money, and he guessed she needed a lot of it with all her adventures. He sincerely hoped Nana hadn't mentioned his real job to this lady.

He tried to focus on her good qualities, but then she'd speak and cause chills to run up his spine. And not the pleasant kind. Maybe she wanted to impress and just went overboard, but he had a bad feeling something much worse lay beneath that bubbly exterior.

Thankfully, the dinner quickly arrived. The chicken curry proved to be the highlight of the night. He tried everything he could think of to finish the date. He paid the waiter and felt profound relief until she spoke again.

"Aren't you going to invite me back to your place?" She fluttered her lashes. "I'd love to spend more time with you."

He bet she would. He wasn't an idjit. "That's a lovely thought, but I have an early day tomorrow."

"That's okay." She purred. "I won't be much of a distraction."

Where did Nana find these women? Sean stepped back to gain distance. He'd had enough of the meddling, blind dates, and constant pressure. He decided to take Cara's advice and create a pretend girlfriend. What did he have to lose at this point?

"Look Sally, I haven't been completely honest." He tried to seem earnest. "I had a girlfriend before I moved to Ireland. We separated due to the distance, but we've recently gotten back together. I'm sorry."

"When your grandmother told my mother about you, she didn't mention any attachments." Her expression darkened, and she glared at him. "What game are you playing? Do you not know who I am?" Her smile turned sinister.

He didn't know her family and didn't care. However, he did want to avoid any further connection to her. "I'm sorry again for the confusion. We broke up before I moved here, so I never mentioned her to my family here. That's the main reason why I kept this date, but she's coming here for a visit, and I'll be introducing her soon." He stood up to avoid any further questions and helped her from the chair.

Her back stiffened, and she narrowed her eyes. "Our families were already discussing possible marriage dates."

"What?" The word exploded out of him before he could control his reaction.

Sally took a step back, and for the first time, acted as if she might believe him. "My family will consider this a personal insult. For the sake of your family, I hope you're telling the truth."

"I am." He felt a little guilty for lying, but he was done with his nana's interference. "My grandmother overstepped but didn't mean any harm." And he'd be having a serious talk with her after this fiasco.

He opened the door of the restaurant and gestured as graciously as he could for Sally to exit.

She jutted out her chin. "We'll see just how much harm has been done." With a huff, she marched out the door and stalked down the street.

"Good riddance, I'd say." Cara stepped up beside him as they passed the entrance to the pub. "She's a nasty piece of work that one."

"Can you lock up tonight?" His weary tone

sounded pathetic, even to his own ears.

Cara squeezed his arm. "Sure. Take a walk and let the fresh, cold air clear your mind."

He took her advice and decided to walk to his family estate. They owned a lot of acreage. His favorite section backed up to a small set of cliffs. They weren't as spectacular as others along the coast, but he'd loved that spot all his life. Every summer he'd spend hours looking out into the unknown, planning all his adventures.

His family home had three stories and a wide footprint. It boasted fifteen bedrooms, eighteen bathrooms, and about every other type of room imaginable. It even had a ballroom and massive dining room. Before his family purchased the property, another developer considered turning it into a hotel. His great-grandfather hadn't wanted to see the historical building become a tourist attraction, so he'd purchased it.

Sean had agreed to stay in the large family home to appease his father. He preferred the small cottage on the north side of the property, near the forested area that he loved, and also not far from the cliffs.

He glanced toward the small home in the distance and noticed lights in the windows. He groaned. He never liked it when Nana rented out the cottage. She always chose some uppity individuals who didn't actually enjoy living in the isolated home. They'd complain the entire stay, and he usually had to deal with them. He'd thought about purchasing the property to protect it and to have a place of his own in Ireland.

He looked one more time at the lights shining in the night and sighed.

I really hope it's not some needy female moving in. I can't take any more.

❄ ❄ ❄

Annie drug her suitcase to the car she'd hired. Once settled in, she hoped to rent her own car and drive herself around. Today, she wanted to get to her destination in one piece. She hadn't been able to sleep on the plane with Mark's words constantly plaguing her.

She eased into the back seat, took a deep breath, and forced herself to focus on the sights as they drove from Dublin airport and headed toward County Clare.

She noticed lots of Christmas decorations and little markets. She decided to ask the driver a few questions to get her research started. "Everything looks so festive and perfect. When do most Irish families decorate for Christmas?"

"Most just decorate when they want these days, but there is an Irish tradition called The Feast of the Immaculate Conception. It occurs on December eighth, and that's when a lot of families decorate. It's a good thing to research. Many families take down decorations on January sixth which is called the Feast of Epiphany. Although, some refer to it as *Little Christmas*. Women will celebrate with a day off. No chores or cooking." He glanced back. "You seem very excited. You're visiting at a grand time of year."

"I'm very interested in all Irish Christmas traditions." Annie watched all the bright colors of the scenery fly by the window.

"We have plenty of fine sights to see." He turned onto a narrow drive that went past a mansion sitting on the left. She had no clue how her manager scored this property, but she'd be getting Sandy an awesome Christmas gift this year. All sorts of ideas for her paintings sped through her mind.

The outside of the cottage had a beautiful yellow hue. It had two stories but a very compact structure. The cute windows were surrounded by white shutters, and the front door had been painted an interesting shade of blue. It felt like she'd entered a faery glen. The yard had been perfectly maintained, and a flower garden had been planted to the side—although not much would be in bloom during the winter. Despite the chill in the air, an overwhelming urge to see the whole property began to build excitement and spread warmth to her cold extremities.

She opened the door to find the décor just as charming. An old farm table sat in the kitchen. The appliances weren't exactly what she used back home, but she'd figure them out and make meals in no time.

She passed a hallway table as she made her way into the living area and breathed a sigh of relief. It had a Wi-Fi password. She didn't feel quite as isolated with that connection to the outside world.

As she continued to the back, she gasped in delight. The cottage had a wonderful sunroom. She'd found the perfect spot to set up her painting supplies. She had shipped a lot of the items to the gallery in Dublin as soon as she'd been chosen for the exhibit. She sent an email to the owner asking if they could send them to her temporary home. She always liked to do final inspections before a showing, and Mark would have her items there within a day or two.

She grabbed her sketchbook and laid it on the table. The driver had given her lots of ideas and Irish traditions to bring to life. However, she'd need personal experience to really bring them to life. She didn't let that temper her excitement. She'd find what she needed.

The upstairs had three small bedrooms. She picked one to sleep in and one for supplies and storage. If Gabby and Mark did come for the exhibit, they'd have plenty of room to stay there. Excitement had her running all over the cottage until she covered every room and had nothing left to put away.

Annie glanced around, then looked at her watch. Her stomach growled, reminding her that she'd had nothing much to eat. The sun wouldn't set for several more hours, and she'd seen a small business area right past the entrance of the property. She could take a walk and grab a bite to eat. Then, she could get a few groceries and essentials.

She hummed as she walked along the narrow path and imagined how beautiful it would be in the spring and summer.

Maybe I'll come back to see it. Her heart raced in anticipation.

As she neared the main road, she noticed a pub to her left named O'Brien's and walked that direction. Once inside, it seemed like a good atmosphere and very tidy. Plenty of seats were available, so she could observe and sketch some of what she'd seen that day.

Annie squared her shoulders and took a deep breath. She had to master doing things on her own and making new acquaintances. She walked farther inside. They had live Irish music that brought a smile to her face. The tune had a happy, uplifting beat. Everyone chatted like old friends.

She had a really good feeling about this place.

Chapter Two

A beautiful woman walked through the door and caught Sean's attention. She looked a little nervous but also had an expression of childish delight. Her long reddish-brown hair caught the rays of sunshine through the window. As she neared, he noticed her bright blue eyes dancing with excitement.

His first reaction to her sparked interest, but irritation quickly followed. If his grandmother had pulled another date fiasco after their talk, he might explode. He watched the lady as she picked a spot at the bar and smiled. She hadn't even glanced his direction.

Guess she's not here for me.

He made his way over to take her order. "What can I get for you?"

Her eyes widened. "You sound American."

"As do you." He smiled and held out his hand. "Born and raised in Indiana."

"I've heard of such a place, but I'm from the mountains of Montana," she teasingly said, then returned his smile and accepted the handshake. "Guess that makes us neighbors in a way."

"You're not wrong." Sean enjoyed her vibrant personality and easy manner. She glowed with excitement. Her eyes actually *twinkled.* He cleared his throat and straightened when he realized he'd been staring at her.

"I arrived early this morning and rented a cottage up the road." Her voice held him captive and created a light buzz in his head. His whole body tingled. He hadn't felt like this since his teen years, and he tried to focus on her words.

"My supplies are limited," she continued, "so I thought I'd grab a bite to eat and get a few items at the market later. What do you recommend from the menu?"

"My favorites are the fish and chips or shepherd's pie, but we also make a good salad if that's more your thing." Sean handed her a menu. "Or we have several other options."

"Hmm." She glanced over the menu. "Both of your favorites sound great. I'll take the shepherd's pie and a water."

"Excellent choice." He started to walk away but turned back. "My name's Sean."

"I'm Annie." She smiled and her eyes crinkled.

A flash of heat traveled up his entire body. "Nice to meet you. Let me put your order in, and we can chat a little more if you'd like." He tried not to sound pushy.

"That would be grand." Annie's smile tilted slightly like she held a big secret. "It's good to know someone around here."

Sean hurried and dropped off the order, then grabbed the water. He didn't want anyone else to capture her attention. He made himself slow down as he approached her. "So, what brings you to Fanore?"

"I'm an artist and working on a project with a gallery in Dublin." She shrugged. "But I'm not much for city life. I like to visit but not stay. I'm more drawn to nature and natural settings. That's what led me here. The scenery is awe-inspiring."

"What type of art do you do?" He didn't want to overwhelm her with questions but found himself wanting to know every aspect of her life.

"I paint. Mostly landscapes, but I've done a wide variety over the years." Annie got a gleam in her eye. "I've got this new idea about holiday traditions. I'd like to start here in Ireland, but I've found it a little difficult to capture real moments when you're an outsider."

He caught himself before he said anything stupid like *spend Christmas with me.* "Which cottage are you renting, if you don't mind me asking? I know most of the folks around here and might be able to help."

"The one past the mansion toward the cliffs." She pointed over her shoulder. "I'm not good with directions, but the property is gorgeous. Do you know the place?"

His heart dropped to his feet. "Yeah, I do. It's part of my family estate. I'm currently living in what you referred to as the *mansion.* I've always loved the little bungalow at the cliffs. You'll have plenty to paint. How long will you be staying?"

"Until Christmas." She drank some of the water. "I have to get back to my family."

Her comment felt like a kick to the teeth. Of course, she'd have a family. "Do you have children?"

"Oh. No." Annie sighed. "No husband. No children. But I do have a brother and sister. We're triplets. They're both married and have children, so Christmas is a big deal for all of us."

"Triplets?" Sean whistled. "That's intense. I'm an only child and can't imagine. Although, I do have a ton of cousins, so I never had the opportunity to feel alone. I always looked forward to my summers here."

"Speaking of family," Cara interrupted him. "I just got a phone call that the whole family is coming for Christmas. All of them. And their children." She shuddered.

"Annie, meet Cara, my cousin." Annie shook her hand. "She's a tad afraid of the young ones."

"My sister, Gabby, just had triplets." Annie laughed when Cara visibly paled. "She's amazing with them. They live on a ranch in Montana. I understand the enormity of mass infants."

"Better you than me." Cara cringed. "You best be believing I have no intentions of such."

"You don't have to convince me." Sean smirked. "But your ma and da are a different story."

She groaned. "Tell me about it." She motioned toward Annie. "I'll go check on your food since this idjit isn't doing anything."

"She's a bundle of energy." Annie watched her

walk away while Cara sung an Irish tune. "And full of confidence. I envy that a little. I'm more the type to hide in my surroundings and sketch them."

"May I see them—if that's allowed?" He pointed at the book by her hand.

"I suppose. But don't judge." She slid it over.

He held up his hand. "I promise."

When he flipped the cover, it took everything he had not to gasp. The intricate detail depicted a perfect scene of his town. She probably only saw some of the aspects on her drive in. He flipped the next page and found an amazing rendition of the cliffs. Page after page reflected the season and life better than a photograph. He'd never witnessed a talent like hers up close.

"These are incredible." He glanced up. "You just arrived this morning. How is this possible?"

"I capture it like a photo in my mind, and then sketch it out," Annie explained. "Of course, these are like rough drafts. I'll create several versions before I choose what to paint. I'm hoping to sketch enough holiday Irish traditions to create a new collection. That's the dream anyway."

Her fingers drew his attention as she closed the book. He wondered how they could create what he'd seen. He'd love to watch her paint, but it might seem a little weird if he asked. Cara arrived with Annie's food, so he gave her some space. He'd monopolized enough of her time. However, he found himself inching back toward her and came up with new topics to discuss. He'd love to know if she had any interest in him the way he did her.

Annie fought to keep her composure as she ate her food. It tasted great, but she felt a little self-conscious with Sean hovering around her. Honestly, he made her nervous. He wore his sandy-colored hair a little long and flipped over the side like he'd run a careless hand through it. His bright-green eyes reminded her of springtime. Green happened to be her favorite color. He stood a good six inches taller than her, and his angular features only strengthened the strong Celtic warrior vibes he exuded.

She ignored the pitter-patter of her heart, needing to focus on art. She didn't have much time to prepare for the Dublin exhibit and formulate her ideas for her next project.

Sean turned to help another customer, but she followed his every move.

What is my fascination with him?

A group of girls burst through the door. They giggled and pointed in Sean's direction, and his expression soured. Annie wondered what had happened between them. She also noticed he didn't go to their table. Cara took their order, and the girls looked disappointed.

Annie tilted her head toward them when Sean walked back over. "Part of the Sean fan club?"

"Not exactly." He sighed. "More like my recurring nightmare."

"*Ouch.* You're gonna have to explain that one." Annie raised her eyebrows. "Don't leave me hanging."

"My family comes from money. When my grandfather passed, my nana made it her mission to see all of her grandchildren married and settled. When I lived in the states, she couldn't really do much damage. When I moved here to help my dad with the pub, she took a new interest in my life. I've been here for months, and the pressure continues to worsen. The blind dates I've been forced to endure are unbelievable. It's become the town joke, hence the silly girls at the table." He frowned toward the girls who were still trying to get his attention.

"Every girl with a pulse and no husband has been after me since Nana began to meddle. The last date I had..." He shook his head. *"Horrific.* Her whole attitude put me on edge, and she acted all uppity and rude. I finally lied and told her I had a girlfriend from the states to make her go away. This is what I've been reduced to. She's already asking around town about the mysterious girl. I'm not sure how long I can hold her off."

"Speaking of..." Cara sidled up to Annie's table and leaned in toward Sean. "Heads up, lover boy. Demon lady and her entourage coming in hot. She's acting particularly combative today."

"Thanks for the warning." Sean grimaced.

Annie felt sorry for him. It made her appreciate her own family even more. They never pushed her without her consent. She couldn't imagine the aggravation the whole thing caused him.

A tall blonde walked in with two of her friends. Their outfits screamed *look at me and I came with a high price tag.* The blonde's chest barely fit in the shirt desperately trying to contain it. They each had expensive pieces of jewelry and reeked of expensive perfume. Blondie leaned against the counter and motioned for Sean to come over.

"Sally, how can I help you?" His harsh tone indicated he didn't want to be anywhere near them. As a business manager, he had to serve his customers, and Annie had to give him props for that.

"Sean," she purred and placed a hand on his arm. "I think you were fibbing about that whole girlfriend business. I've asked around, and no one seems to remember you ever mentioning her. If you're shy, that's okay. I'll take care of you." Her sickly-sweet voice made Annie want to vomit.

"I can take care of myself." Sean stepped back. "And I assure you my girlfriend is real. She simply doesn't need to be in the spotlight or around drama."

"You're lying." The woman became angrier, and fire flashed in her eyes. "I have a lot of power in this county, and I could destroy your effing pub."

"My family is connected as well, so your threats mean little." Sean crossed his arms. "This is causing a scene, so please leave."

Her face turned an ugly shade of red, and her whole demeanor darkened. Annie sensed a lot of issues bottled up in the woman. "No one tells me to leave, especially not a pathetic liar." She grabbed his arm and dug in her nails.

"That's enough!" Annie stormed around the counter. The rational side of her brain screamed at her to stop, but she'd been raised to stand with friends, and Sean felt like a potential friend.

"Who are you?" Disdain dripped from every syllable Sally uttered.

"I'm the girlfriend you're so determined to find." Annie reached forward and removed Sally's hand from Sean's arm. "He wanted to protect me and keep it quiet. But I guess there's no point now. You need to leave and take your pack with you."

Annie put her arm around Sean's waist and brushed her lips across his ear. "Play along," she whispered.

Sean's ear tingled from Annie's warm breath. He didn't wait for Annie to change her mind and slid an arm around her back, then pulled her close. "As you can see, I told the truth, Sally."

"I bet you did." Sally snarled and glared at Annie. "If you're his girlfriend, prove it. Let's see a kiss between the two of you." She sneered like she'd outwitted them.

Sean froze. He knew he should let Annie off the hook and confess the truth. He wouldn't allow her to be forced into kissing a stranger when she'd only tried to help. His conscious yelled at him to end the act.

"Fine." Annie took away his decision. Her eyes met Sally's in total determination. "I find this very inappropriate, but dealing with you bothers me more. I'll do what it takes to shut you up."

Sean still hesitated, but Annie met his eyes and gave an imperceptible nod. She reached up on her toes, and he dipped down to meet her. His stomach flopped and his palms were sweaty. Their first touch sent electricity straight to his heart and left him wanting so much more. Without thought, he tightened his grip and pulled her closer. She melted beneath him, and he lost any sense of his surroundings.

His heart began to hammer, and all he could hear was the blood pumping in his ears. He had run out of air and didn't care. His thoughts were scattered, but he knew he didn't want to let her go.

The pub erupted with applause from the customers and broke the spell. He pulled back but still held her close.

"I think that's your cue to leave," Annie snipped and crossed her arms, yet she didn't leave his embrace. "I'd appreciate it if you didn't return. He's mine."

Annie nodded toward the door, and then stared at Sally until she began to move to the exit.

Before the door shut, Sally stuck her head back inside. "You'll regret this. That's a promise."

Annie made no retort. She simply raised her eyebrows and shrugged like she didn't care. Sally slammed the door hard enough to rattle the walls.

"I don't know how to thank you for what you just did." Sean took Annie's hand and led her into the back office, away from prying eyes and ears. "I hope she doesn't cause you any trouble."

"If she tries, I'll call my sister." Annie laughed. "That will be the end of that. I've dealt with her type many times over the years, especially when protecting my brother. Don't worry about it."

Annie walked back to her seat and sat down. She kept her head tilted down and had clearly become uncomfortable. The other customers watched her every move. Sean followed her and racked his brain on how to fix things. She'd never get any peace in this small town now. He doubted she'd visit the pub again, not after what happened the first time she walked in. His family would make things worse once they heard the news.

Unless...

An idea began to form in his mind. They had both already lied about having a relationship in a pretty flamboyant manner. What if they kept the ruse going for a little longer? He only had a month left until his dad returned to full time, and one of his cousins returned from London in February. He'd be the one eventually taking over the pub. All Sean needed was a girlfriend to help him out for a few weeks, and Annie needed a guide for holiday traditions.

"Listen," he whispered and leaned in front of her. "I have a crazy idea to help both of us."

She raised one eyebrow. "Really? I've already pretended to be your girlfriend and kissed a stranger. How much crazier are we talking?"

"You mentioned your next project is all about Irish Christmas traditions. You need a personal connection to really experience all there is to see and know. I can give you that. And I can be your personal guide. With Dad coming back part-time, I have more freedom. We can do all the activities, and you can sketch everything. It's a win-win."

"What's the catch for this generous offer you're proposing?" Annie warily asked and tilted her head back.

"I need for you to keep being my pretend girlfriend until the holiday season is over. By then, I'll be preparing my move back to the states, or wherever I decide to go next. I'll always love Ireland but it's become a tad suffocating. I'm afraid my nana will hinder the time I have left with her matchmaking schemes if I don't find a sort of shield against her efforts. We can help each other. What do you say?"

"I don't know." Her features scrunched up, and she seemed distressed by the idea. "It doesn't feel right to lie to your family."

"If you think about, how much are we deceiving them?" Sean reasoned. "We'll be doing all sorts of dating activities and sight-seeing stuff. We just know the outcome ahead of time. Honestly, I think this might be the easiest and best relationship I've ever had."

"Hmm..." Annie's expression softened. "You make a good point, and I desperately need a guide to get all my material for my paintings." She tapped a finger against her sketch book. "We'd have to set some ground rules and create a believable, yet simple, story. Cara knows the truth about us, so she'd have to be okay with all this, too."

"This whole thing was actually her idea." Annie couldn't look more confused. "She suggested the whole pretend thing before I met you," Sean explained. "I didn't think it was possible, but then you walked into the pub. We can set whatever rules you want. Is it a deal?"

Sean's eyes pleaded for Annie to say yes, and a large part of her wanted to agree to the absurd arrangement. And it was definitely absurd, to say the least. She couldn't even count all the possible things that could go wrong.

He appeared to be a good man and well liked, but she didn't know him or his family. But he could certainly kiss, and that counted for a lot in her book.

Her mind drifted back to her conversations with Gabby. She'd taken a chance on Jake. Both her siblings had faced challenges and surprises. Maybe it was her turn.

What if she failed?

Her heartbeat sped up and brought a churning into her stomach. She hadn't let Gabby be a coward, so she couldn't be one herself. Gabby and Mark would never let her forget it.

A big, *danger* sign flashed in her head. The risk carried a lot of potential for heartache, but he offered everything she needed to make her newest project a success. He couldn't hurt her if she already knew the score. Her world revolved around art and that would never change.

She returned her full focus to his gorgeous green eyes. "It's a deal." She held out her hand, and he took it. Her fingers tingled from his touch, and she had a bad feeling none of this would be as simple as they thought.

"I'll fill in Cara after we close tonight." Sean nodded in his cousin's direction. "She'll support us."

"What do we tell everyone?" Annie fidgeted with her pencils. The constant stares made her self-conscious. "I mean other than the kiss, no one has seen us together, nor do we have any type of history."

"We need to keep it simple," Sean said. "How about we met at an art gallery in the states and dated a few times? I had to leave to help my dad when he had his big fall from the ladder, and we weren't sure about long-distance relationships. We stayed in touch and decided to give it another go with me returning soon. You visited me due to your art show and to spend the holidays together."

"Sounds simple enough." Annie sighed. Everything always sounded simple in the beginning. "Did your dad actually fall from a ladder?"

"Yeah, but he's getting better."

"Good, I'm glad to know that. Still, if your family is anything like mine, they'll ask questions like how *exactly* did we meet, where did we go for our first date, and more. I don't want you to tell one story and me another."

"Okay, let's meet up tomorrow and hash out some of the most likely questions. Most of the time we'll be together and can take turns with answers." He pointed at some paper. "We each make a list of places and activities that sound like us. The holidays are a crazy time around here, so my family will be distracted and not as curious as usual. That gives us a little more space. Plus, I don't go around kissing strangers, so my family is already on board with the two of us."

"If you're sure." Annie still didn't like the deception regarding his family, but he had made an excellent point that they would actually be dating in a roundabout way. "I feel a little guilty."

"I'm headed out after the new year, and you're

leaving after Christmas." Sean shrugged. "How much interaction will we have with them?"

"I guess." Annie frowned. "Will your grandmother be okay when all is revealed?"

"Oh yeah." Sean smirked. "A tanker can't take that lady down. She'll be just fine and trying to find me a new wife in no time."

"Fair point." Annie laughed. "So, tomorrow morning?" Annie took out some money to pay for her food.

"I'll be at your cottage around eight." He pushed the money back to her. "You don't owe me anything. You can eat here as often as you want and order whatever you like. I'm still in your debt, and this is the least I can provide."

His generosity touched her. She promised herself not to take him up on the offer too often. "See you then."

Annie headed out as the last few rays of sunshine glistened across the town. Good thing she'd brought her heavy coat. The air had gained quite a chill to it, and she still had to walk back.

A few doors down, she discovered a small market and stepped inside. She moved up and down the aisles and picked up some new foods to try. She grabbed some staples like milk, eggs, and butter. The veggies beckoned to her, so she added a green pepper, onion, and a few others. Her hands would be full, but she'd carry it all.

Sean had promised to drop by in the morning, so she had to figure out all those appliances. They were dated compared to the new stainless steel that Mark had installed in her cabin. Omelets and juice would be enough to tide them over while they plotted out their fake relationship.

She shook her head as she stepped into the frosty air. What had she gotten herself into? Gabby would get a kick out of it, but Annie hoped her new Christmas series would be worth the potential disaster that could ensue.

The path veered into the edge of the trees. The sun had begun to give way to the soft glow of the moon. She had just enough light left to get inside the cottage before the night sky darkened her little corner of the world.

She went in and put the groceries on the kitchen counter, then felt compelled to step through the back door and into the back gardens. She gasped in delight, grateful she'd followed her instincts.

The moon towered over the cliffs, creating a spectacular display of reflections and shadows. She grabbed her camera and took several shots. That scene would become a future painting. It just needed another element to make it complete.

She headed back inside to tackle her next challenge.

"This is ridiculous," Annie muttered to herself.

So far, she'd managed to burn four eggs and waste some of her milk. If she didn't figure out how to master the blasted stove, they'd have to eat snacks for breakfast. Her third attempt went much better but still lacked her usual perfection. At least the omelet was edible, so she ate it for dinner.

Her phone rang. "Hey Gabby. I started to call but remembered the time difference. How are the babies?"

"My trio of trouble are doing fine." Gabby laughed. "If you don't count spitting up and pooping on the carpet—Jake's mistake on the last one—and our usual lack of sleep, we're all doing great. It's lunchtime for me. I miss you, and so do the kiddos."

"I miss you all." Annie sighed. "Even Mark. I can't believe I missed Jake's face for that mishap. Mark sent pictures of Nate in Santa's lap. It makes me sad to not be there with you."

"You're where you should be," Gabby reassured her. "I'll take lots of pictures and videos. We'll have a good laugh when you get home because, yes, I even caught the end of Jake's fiasco. It's a must see. Also, Mark and I spoke with Jake and Ally about your art show. They both agreed that we should be there for you this year as you've been there for us over the last two years. Mark booked flights. We'll still be together for Christmas then come home to celebrate with the whole family. You should know that Jake and Ally insisted on this. They love you, too."

"Oh, Gabby." Annie choked back the tears and cleared her throat. "You can't leave your children for their first Christmas."

"Don't be silly, Annie." Gabby's soft voice brought Annie comfort. "The babies have no idea what the day will be. Neither does Nate. We'll have a big celebration when we return and none will be the wiser. It's your turn to shine, and we've always stood behind you. Nothing will change that."

Emotions made it hard for Annie to speak. She had to change the subject or risk a total meltdown. She decided to tell her about the crazy day she'd had instead. "You'll never believe what I did today..." She filled Gabby in about Sean, his grandmother, and the steamy kiss.

"Wow, that's pretty out there, especially for you." Gabby paused. "But I'd say that qualifies as a clear sign. The triplet decree mandates that you follow all opportunities. Wild or not, I think the pretend relationship might be good for you. Even if he's not *the one,* this could lead to the one that is."

Gabby's words replayed in Annie's mind as she drifted off to sleep. She needed a man willing to travel all over the world and love her family as much as she did. A tall order. She didn't even know if such a man existed, but she wouldn't settle for less.

Chapter Three

"What the..." Sean pulled up behind a large moving van.

I thought she's only here a couple weeks.

He followed the delivery guy into the house where several large square packages had been placed around the living area. A few had been opened. Curiosity got the better of him and he moved closer to take a look. Astonishment knocked him back on his heels. He had a strange feeling he'd seen art pieces like them before. He recognized the landscapes and style of the artist.

It can't be.

Annie entered the room and stared at him. Her eyes were wide as if she worried what he'd think, or that he'd recognized her work. "You're here earlier than I thought. I had hoped to have these cleared out of the way before you arrived. I'm using one of the bedrooms upstairs as a storage area until I double-check all of the paintings and have them sent to the gallery."

"Wait... Wait..." He stuttered. "You're *the* Annabella Duncan? Worldwide famous artist? I've seen your work in many galleries. You have the uncanny ability to make people feel like they're in the paintings—like I can feel the breeze when I'm looking at one. They're so real. Is that you?"

She hesitated, then nodded. "I go by Annie and that's how my friends know me. I use Annabella for my official title for shows. My brother and sister believed the full name gave the pieces more flare with an exotic name. Not sure if it did all that, but it does provide some distance at times. So, I can be just Annie."

"Your intense sketches make a lot more sense now." He'd been a huge fan of her work for years and had purchased several pieces. He'd also seen one of her Irish landscapes at the Dublin gallery. The morning mists above the cliffs had surrounded him as he stood staring at the piece. It had given him chills and stayed with him.

"Hold up." He faced her again. "Siblings. You mean the novelist, Marcus Duncan and the book cover graphic designer, Gabriella Duncan? You three are triplets?"

"Yep." She grinned, but her eyes held suspicion. "My secret's out. That's us. The famous Duncan triplets. Although, we all enjoy the quiet life in Montana. Our town allows us to be normal and protects us, when necessary, from crazy fans. I can't believe you've heard of all three of us." She inched closer. "I'd like to keep this between us. I don't want a lot of attention as I prepare."

"I won't say anything. Nana instilled the love of art into me at an early age." He smiled. "She even quizzed us. She's one of the main benefactors of the Dublin gallery exhibiting your work. There's no way she won't recognize you. She does her research. We'll need to consider that, but she'll be discreet and understand."

"At least that goes along with the story we're creating." Annie moved toward the table. "It would explain why I'm here, and why we wanted to keep things quiet. The appreciation of art explains your knowledge of me, but what about Gabby and Mark?"

"As much as Nana loved art, Grandad loved his Celtic heritage." Sean thought about all the memories of his grandad's love of smoking a pipe and telling stories of faeries and magic. "He always had a new story or myth to share until he passed. His stories sparked a world of curiosity for me. I began to read science fiction and fantasy even more so after he died. I met your brother at a couple Comic Cons, and who I'm assuming is your sister because—now that I think about it—you two look a lot alike. Funny, the two of us never met. Where were you?"

"I was there." She sighed and sat on the edge of the table. "Crowds have always been a challenge for me, but it never fazed Gabby. She'd be the face pushing us along, and as you know, her book covers are legendary. What I can do with my paints and canvas, she can do with a computer. I prefer the background and would organize and plan. Gabby did the same for me as she did for Mark. She attended all my shows and never let anyone see a chink in my armor. I'm here to learn to do more on my own. I can't lean on her forever even if she'd let me. I think I need to prove to myself that I can do it."

"You're off to a good start. You even gained a boyfriend on your first day here." He bumped her shoulder.

She snorted. "I'm not sure that goes in the responsible column, and your worthiness remains to be seen."

"Touché." He laughed and followed her into the kitchen. She had several mixing bowls lying on the counters. "However, your paintings are amazing. No doubt."

"I decided to make us some breakfast to go with our discussion." She gestured around the kitchen, explaining all the bowls. "I prepared some omelets. They're mixed and ready to pour into the skillets. I spent an hour last night figuring out how to work the blasted stove."

She glanced over her shoulder. "I thought we could create a list of traditions I need to observe most. We can check them off as we complete them, and it keeps us focused since my time is limited."

"We have a lot of traditions." Sean took a seat at the table and grabbed a smaller piece of paper. "I'll jot several of them down, and you can turn it into a pretty list later."

"I'm good with that." Annie poured the eggs into the pan. "What are some of your favorites, or what's most popular?"

"A biggie is the Feast of Immaculate Conception.

It traditionally takes place on December eighth, but some vary the date now depending on other factors, like family." Sean wrote the details. "It's also the day when many families decorate, even though quite a few families decorate earlier these days. Still, it's a notable tradition and an excuse to throw a party."

He wrote a few more things into the notes while she tended the food.

"What else do you recommend?" Annie put one omelet on a plate and poured the next into the pan.

"You have to check out all the Christmas markets. Killarney has an amazing outdoor setup, but my favorite is Galway. They turn Eyre square into a magical Christmas wonderland. Dublin has quite a few as well that we need to see. I have the late shift at the pub tonight, so we could check one out today if you have time. I suggest Galway."

"Terrific." Annie laid a plate in front of him that smelled like heaven. He held in a groan of satisfaction. The woman could cook as well as she painted. At least with eggs.

She sat down beside him. "My schedule is clear. I have to inspect the paintings for the gallery over the next day or two, so they're ready for delivery. Otherwise, I'm free. Galway is one of the places I loved during my quick trip last year, but we were more focused on the more notable sites for my landscapes."

"Galway it is." He dug into his food and savored every bite. They passed the next few minutes in silence while they ate their meal.

"What else do you suggest?" Annie pushed her plate to the side.

"Are you done with that?" He pointed at her half-eaten omelet.

Annie nodded, so Sean pushed her remaining food onto his plate. "Midnight Mass on Christmas Eve is widely observed. There's the Christmas Day Swim which is a forty-foot jump into frigid waters if you're more adventurous."

"I think I'll pass on hypothermia for now," Annie drawled. "Anything a little less dangerous on the list?"

"Everyone loves to meet Santa, and some areas still do Christmas caroling, but it's mostly for charities now." Sean thought for a minute. "Oh, I've got a good one. Ugly sweater contests. They're hideous and loved by the Irish. We have a contest in our pub. People even walk up to strangers and compete on the streets. There's also the light in the window to welcome family home. There are parties almost every night of the week. The possibilities are endless."

"I'm ready if you are." Annie jumped up and put their dishes in the sink. She grabbed her coat and motioned for him to follow. "The delivery guys are gone, so we can head out. I'm excited to see it all."

Her enthusiasm fed his own. He found himself laughing and running after her. He hadn't felt this kind of carefree happiness in a long time. Not since his mother passed. Annie chattered all the way to Galway. Her love for all things Christmas became apparent and she kept him entertained with stories of her past. She squealed the moment they came close and the market appeared in the distance. Her face pressed against the glass like a child's. She made him feel the same—full of hope and dreams.

He opened her car door and helped her out, then held onto her hand and laced their fingers together. She didn't pull away, so either she thought it was part of the pretend relationship or she enjoyed his touch. He'd take either one. If things continued to work out, maybe they could redefine some of the *pretend* aspects.

Annie's heart nearly leapt out of her chest when Sean took her hand. A spark radiated up her entire arm.

If only this was real.

She forced the thought from her mind and decided to make the most of their time together. Not everyone got a forever relationship. Some had to settle for right now.

"Oh look!" She spotted a little booth full of artwork and handmade jewelry. "Gabby loves Celtic symbols. I have to buy her a piece for Christmas."

"Don't you want to look around a little? There's lots to see." Sean's distraught expression made her laugh. He had no idea what he'd walked into.

"I'm just getting the necklace." She patted his cheek. "Relax. Have some fun. I won't make you carry too many packages." She rushed off to the next table, pulling him behind her. He groaned but didn't say anything else. She took pictures of everything as they went from place to place.

"It smells delicious." Annie took a deep breath. "What is it?"

"They're serving mulled wine and minced pies

for the adults. Hot chocolate and pastries for the kids." Sean pointed at another area. "They have the most amazing French delicacies and up a little farther, you can sample some Irish whiskies."

If she wasn't careful, she'd gain fifty pounds during her visit. "This place is massive." Annie turned around in a circle to take it all in.

"They usually have over sixty chalets, or booths, as you call them. Performers are here almost every night." He guided her forward and pointed in the distance. "Santa's Grotto is over there, and they even bring in rides for the children. I'll have to bring you back one night when it's all lit up. There's nothing like it."

Annie sensed the awe in his voice. He loved this country more than he realized. She absorbed the sounds of Christmas magic and music and imagined how it would be with all the lights twinkling. She'd be back to see it.

"What else is here?"

Sean motioned to another area. "There's an ice-skating rink in that part and a stage for live performances over there. Countries from all over participate in the festival. It's only open about six weeks but brings in over six-hundred-thousand visitors. Galway gets a huge economic boost from all the traffic."

"Look at you." Annie narrowed her eyes. "All analytical. I see the financial manager coming out. I am glad Galway gets a revenue boost. I want to know more about the people, performers. Their life and their talents." Another table caught her attention because it had lots of ribbon and color.

"What about the chalet over there?"

"Wreath-making." Sean started to walk in that direction. "A huge tradition in Ireland."

"How so?" Annie followed him to the sweet lady selling and making the beautiful wreaths.

"Long ago, some of the less fortunate citizens, used holly wreaths to decorate. They could gather the supplies and create holiday decorations. The trend grew, and now it's a thing." Sean smiled. "My family has a ton of them. One for every door in the house. You can make your own here."

She turned and grabbed his arm. "Can we make one?"

"You're the artist." Sean moved aside for her to take a seat, and then joined her. "I'll watch while you create."

"No, you'll *help*." Annie handed him some supplies.

"You sure about that?" Sean grimaced. "I'm pretty bad at all things creative."

"Anyone can do art." Annie picked up some branches and began weaving. "You just have to be willing and patient." She turned and caught him staring at her. It made her nervous to think he might be interested in her as well.

They spent the next half hour adding ribbon and perfecting the design. Annie loved the result. She'd place it on her front door as soon as she got back to the cottage. After they finished, she continued to browse all the small businesses and artisans. She sampled plenty of food and sweets. She imagined setting up her own chalet and selling miniatures. This place offered solace and a home away from home. She planned to return many times, but since Sean would go back to his other life, she'd be alone.

She shook it off. Nothing could ruin this experience.

Sean's phone rang, and he answered. Someone quickly spoke on the other end. Annie couldn't quite make out the words. "Tonight? Are you kidding?" He listened for a bit. "I'll ask but won't pressure." Another pause. "Fine. See you tonight."

"What's wrong?" Annie recognized the crease between his brows and got a bad feeling.

"That was Cara." He jerked his hands through his hair. "Nana has decided that we're having a feast tonight since the rest of the family arrived this morning. She even called in someone to cover my shift tonight."

"That doesn't sound too bad." Annie always looked forward to family dinners.

"She demanded that you attend as well." His face flushed red with embarrassment. "I'm sorry to throw this on you."

Her first reaction was to decline. Things had already gotten complicated, but she'd agreed to be his shield against his grandmother's matchmaking. Sean spent the entire day in Galway helping her, so she had to return the favor. No matter how awkward it turned out.

"That's what we agreed to, so I'm game." She tried to sound positive. "I'd love to go and meet your family." Some of that spiel had a grain of truth somewhere.

"I guess we better head back." Sean had become deflated and lost the joy that had been in his eyes.

"Do we still have time to grab groceries?" Annie tentatively asked. "I can be quick. I'm only here for a few weeks, and I love to cook. I'd like to do a big trip while I have a car available to carry it. It will also allow me to make cookies tonight. I have a great recipe and would like to contribute."

"One condition." His smile returned, and he leaned toward her.

"What?" she suspiciously asked.

"You use some of the food and especially cookies to feed me." He bumped her shoulder as they walked. "I love home-cooked meals and if you cook like those omelets you made this morning, I'll be eating good. And I'll tell you about our cookie tradition."

"I'm all ears." Annie couldn't wait to hear more about Ireland and to experience a family celebration.

"Biscuits and cookies are the same thing here?" Annie's confused expression made Sean laugh. Her stormy, blue eyes held him captive, but he reminded himself it wasn't real.

"Sort of, but not like the ones you made." Sean picked up a cookie shaped like a star and bit off the edge. "Man, these are good. I'd be a thousand pounds if I cooked like this." He licked the icing off his fingers.

"Okay, so explain this box of biscuits tradition." Annie gave him a stern look when he reached for another cookie. He gave her his best puppy-dog expression and snagged another one.

"It's basically the same and includes shortbreads, bourbon creams, tea biscuits, soda cookies, and lace cookies. Really, you can do any combination that you choose. The usual tradition is to include ten types of cookies." Sean eyed another cookie, but Annie snatched the tray away and covered it.

"Why ten?" Annie stacked another set of cookies into the tray.

"I'm sure there's a reason, but I don't know. A family places each type of cookie by layer and stacks them. Each layer represents one flavor or type. The story goes that one layer must be finished before the next can be touched. Families would fight over who got which cookie." Sean dried some of the dishes to help Annie clean up. "My family considers it more of a free-for-all and grab whatever. I have a feeling your cookies will be a huge hit."

"I hope so." Annie washed the last dish. "If you can finish this, I'll go change for the party."

"Sure, I've got it." Sean watched her hurry up the stairs. A piece of him felt like he needed to take a step back. They had become very domesticated, and he struggled to remember that none of it was real. If he wasn't careful, he'd fall hard for the woman who reminded him of a faery princess. She moved in a regal manner but with the energy of a small child. She fascinated him.

Her return steps signaled the time had come to face his family. He moved toward her and froze. Gone were the leggings and long shirt. She'd traded them in for a fitted, dark-green dress that stopped mid-thigh. The thin straps showcased her shoulders until she placed a wrap around them. She'd slipped on heels and braided her hair into a complicated pattern to complete the transformation.

"Ready?" She waved in front of his face. "Sean?"

"Yeah, let's go." He picked up her jacket and slid it over her. His thoughts had scattered again. He briefly wondered what she'd do if he swept her up into his arms and kissed her. He just might try it later.

She picked up the cookies and walked out the door. A light drizzle began to fall, so they hurried to his car. They didn't speak the short drive to his home. He figured her nerves were on edge and his weren't much better.

"Listen..." Sean said as they reached his long, curving driveway. "My relatives can be loud and crazy. You're new, so they'll be very attentive and curious. I wanted to apologize up front."

She patted his leg. "Don't worry. I can handle it..." Her voice trailed when he parked in front of the massive, three-story building that he called home. When he saw it through her eyes, the stonework gave him chills. Several stained-glass windows stretched across the front. It boasted a large garage to one side, and the gardens stretched beyond the home.

The grandeur surprised him at times. Annie took pictures of everything and asked a lot of questions. She gasped as they entered the grand front hall. On the left, the massive dining room had been decorated for tonight's dinner. He took her into the living area, and she gasped again and stopped in her tracks in front of the fireplace.

He finally understood what had captured her attention. It wasn't the enormity of the fireplace, but rather, what hung above the mantel: one of Annie's art pieces. It had been one of his favorites for years. He knew it was set in Alaska due to the northern lights illustrated perfectly in the picture. In the center, stood a well. Light exploded from the depths and cast shadows over three figures hidden in the light. He'd stared at this painting more than he'd ever admit.

"Annabella, it's wonderful to meet you." Nana approached Annie. Her green eyes shined with mischief, but she smiled and held out her hand. Sean hadn't known what to expect.

"Please call me Annie." Annie accepted Nana's outstretched hand.

"I'm Ava O'Brien. Call me Ava or Nana if you'd like." She nervously glanced at Sean. "You're probably not very happy with me. I wouldn't have interfered if I had known about you. My grandson doesn't share much."

"That's quite all right," Annie reassured her. "It's been difficult for us to build a relationship. I travel so much, and he's needed here. When the art gallery invited me, we felt it was a sign."

"That we did." Sean placed his arm around Annie's waist and felt a slight tremble. Guilt washed over him. Despite her bravado, without a doubt, Annie felt uncomfortable. "Nana, we've been on our feet most of the day, and I'm starved. What's for dinner?"

Nana looped her arm though his. "All your favorites. I must admit I can't wait to try one of Annie's lovely cookies. They smell divine."

"And taste better." Sean used his free hand and grasped Annie's. She smiled at him and his heart stuttered. He pulled her close and ignored the warning signs that he could be getting in too deep. "Let's go eat."

"It's about time you brought your girl to meet the family." Sean's dad walked up to them as they entered the dining area.

"Nice to meet you." Annie held out her hand. "I'm Annie Duncan.

"I've heard all about you from my friends at the pub." He chuckled when Annie's face flushed. "I'm Patrick. Pleased to meet you."

Sean's father introduced her to many other family members until Sean figured Annie's head spun with the endless names and relations. He tried to steer her to safety. Finally, they sat at the table and began passing around all of his favorite dishes.

When all bellies were full, several of Sean's family picked up instruments and began to play a mix of Irish tunes and Christmas carols.

Cara pulled Annie to the center of the floor. She attempted to teach Annie an infamous Irish step-dance that many Sean knew referred to as *Riverdance*. It didn't go well. Annie ended up bruising Cara's shins. It was a blast to watch the whole thing unfold. Sean had never laughed so hard in his life. Several other family members twirled Annie around the room until she returned to him.

The music slowed and Sean pulled Annie against him. She fit perfectly tucked against him, and they swayed to the soft beat. Sean met her eyes and smiled. In that moment, he handed over his heart. He didn't know how it happened or why, but he'd fallen hard in no time. Yet, to have any shot at all with her, he needed to convince Annie the feelings were real. Did he tell her now or give it more time? He didn't want her to run away.

She laid her head on his shoulder and his thoughts went to the future and all they could be. He decided to tell her when the time was right.

Annie's heart hammered in exhilaration. Sean's arms wrapped around her and the rest of the world disappeared. She hadn't planned on losing her heart when she'd agreed to Sean's plan. What did she do now? She could walk away, but what would that prove? She heard Gabby's voice in her head, reminding her to take the chance. The same lecture she'd given to Gabby about Jake. She'd witnessed the love between them and Mark and Ally. It didn't take a genius to see she'd fallen for Sean.

Her head wanted her to tell Sean and end the fake relationship. Her heart wanted more time. The debate raged in her mind until the sway of their bodies quieted her thoughts. Warmth spread through her entire body. Even if the time with Sean couldn't be forever, she'd take the time fate had given her and appreciate it. He never needed to know that he'd captured her heart from his first hello.

"Need some air?" Sean whispered.

Annie nodded and took his hand. He led her into the back gardens. The shining moon bathed the area in a soft white light. Pure magic. Annie didn't have any other words to describe it. "It's all so breath-taking."

"It's pretty amazing." Sean wrapped his arms around her.

"Your family is great." Annie glanced up at him. "I still feel a little guilty but thankful all the same. It makes not having my family here with me a little easier."

Sean smiled and tucked a stray hair behind her ear. "They all like you, too. Nana even asked if you'd be our guest for Saint Stephen's Day. It's a huge family tradition for us."

"I'm not familiar with that one." Annie crinkled her brow.

"It's a day of horse races in South Dublin on the day after Christmas." Sean grinned. "Basically, it provides Nana with a chance to socialize with all her friends, but it can also be entertaining."

"It sounds amazing, but I leave Christmas morning," Annie reminded him.

His smile faded. "Right. I almost forgot we're on a timeline."

The magical moment between them passed. He stiffened and put a little distance between them. She'd do well to remember the reality of the situation.

"I'll drive you home." She followed Sean back inside, and he grabbed her coat. "It's too cold to walk and a little late. Plus, I feel rain coming."

His irritation concerned her. What did he have to be upset about? It may have dawned on him that he'd eventually have to tell his family the truth.

Things sure had gotten messy. He helped her into his car, and they drove the short distance to the cottage in silence.

Annie unlocked her cottage door and Sean reached out for her hand. "Annie, wait. I'm sorry I got a little moody. It's tricky with my family and everything."

"I know." Annie squeezed his hand. "I don't like deceiving them either."

He nodded and tilted his head to the side. "Are we still on for the Christmas markets in Dublin tomorrow?"

"Of course." Annie grinned. "I can't wait, and I need my guide. I've read all about them. Tomorrow night, Cara is taking me to a live performance in Galway that she says I have to experience. I'm making enough memories to last a lifetime. I'll see you tomorrow. Goodnight." She refused to have any regrets.

"Tomorrow." He nodded. "Goodnight." They locked eyes for a moment, then he walked away. She shut the door and leaned against it.

Her phone dinged, and she looked at the pictures Cara had sent. Some were portraying her awful attempt at dance, but several represented the whole family. The last one Cara had taken without her knowing. She and Sean were standing outside bathed in the moonlight. His face angled toward hers, while her face had an upward tilt to meet his. Their eyes locked in a long gaze. His arm encircled her waist as she leaned into his larger frame. To any outsider, the two people in the picture looked totally in love.

The reality broke her heart. She'd dreamed of finding that spark all her life. Instead, she'd been given a glimpse, and it would disappear after Christmas. With her mind heavy, she sat down in front of a large blank canvas and expressed her deepest desire the only way she knew how.

Her brush strokes flowed with ease as she captured the scene and brought it to life.

This could be my finest work yet.

Chapter Four

"The lighthouses were beautiful." Annie sighed. "I've always loved them. I think I'll sketch a few for my private collection."

Sean glanced in her direction. He admired her love of life and simple pleasures. She brought happiness wherever she went. He'd researched many of her pieces, and each one held a warmth that similarly radiated to the beacons that inspired her.

Annie continued to gush over their time at the Rock of Cashel and some other sites in Dublin. She'd stopped in at the gallery for a meeting, and they'd dropped off a few of her pieces. It allowed him to see some of her work. Breathtaking didn't accurately describe the beauty. She seemed too good to be real. Why had she picked him and agreed to this ridiculous scheme when she had the world at her fingertips?

"What's up with all the little lights in the windows?" Annie broke his concentration.

"What do you mean?" Sean tried to redirect his thoughts.

"Several of the buildings and homes that we pass all have a candle or some type of light. I wondered about the significance. Is it what you mentioned to me before about welcoming family home? I'd like to include that in one of my traditions if it fits."

"Yes, it's mostly to welcome people home whether it's family or strangers." Sean paused and tried to remember some of Nana's stories. "Many still observe the tradition and place a light in the window on Christmas Eve. However, most have a light the entire holiday season. An interesting fact, one of Ireland's presidents from the nineties displayed a permanent candle in the window of Aras and Uachtarain. She re-adopted the custom to remember all of the Irish immigrants and hoped it would show them the way back home."

"That's a lovely story." Annie smiled. "What was her name? I may incorporate her into the painting."

"Mary Robinson." Sean scratched his head. "I don't remember much else except my Nana had a lot of respect for her. That says a lot. She's hard to impress."

"Don't I know it." Annie shuddered. "I feel like she's looking straight through me at times. Like she can see my deepest secrets. It can be intimidating."

"She has that effect on everyone." Sean laughed. "Including me. However, she only has positive things to say about you."

"I can't believe over a week has passed." Annie gazed from her window as he pulled into the drive of her cottage. "My exhibit is in a couple days. Time has flown by."

Her soft words were like a sucker punch to his gut. He didn't want her to leave. They had bonded over the silliest of Irish traditions, but now each one had a memory of her attached to it. He'd never be able to celebrate Christmas without thoughts of Annie and her infectious laughter. It pulled at his heart more than he wanted to admit. Their whole relationship had been based on a scam, but it didn't feel pretend. He enjoyed every second in her company.

He helped her inside with all her packages. Cinnamon and sugar overtook his sense of smell and his stomach growled. Between Annie's unique, spicy personal scent and the aroma of her cooking, Sean wanted to stay indefinitely. He glanced in her direction as she bustled around the kitchen to make tea and grab cookies. The sleek movements of her body had his own tied in knots. His feelings for her grew each day. Truth hit hard. He avoided any talk of her leaving, but that wouldn't change the facts.

He wouldn't ask her to stay longer. She had a family and friends waiting for her. A home and place she loved. He wondered if she realized how much love she held in her heart for that ranch in Montana. She talked of traveling, but she'd never stay separated from her siblings for long. They had a bond he couldn't fathom. Why would she choose him over all that?

Annie placed the cup and a plate in front of him. "You've grown quiet. Anything wrong?"

He wanted to tell the truth but figured it might be a little much to digest, so he went with evasive. "Just thinking."

"Okay." The smile she cast didn't quite reach her eyes.

He wished he could read her mind to see if she felt the same as he did. Since that wasn't possible, he decided to distract her and learn a little more about her life.

"Tell me about the infamous wishing well. You've mentioned it several times but no details." She glanced up in surprise. "I've also seen some of the sketches. I sense more to the story."

For a moment, she just looked at him, and he didn't think she'd respond. Then she sighed and shook her head. "It's quite unbelievable. I'll tell you if you promise not to judge."

He crossed his heart and held up his hand. "Promise."

"It took place when Gabby, Mark, and I were young, and we lived in North Pole, Alaska."

"Wait a minute." Sean interrupted. "You lived at the North Pole. Seriously?"

"Yep." She grinned. "And it was a magical place for kids. The three of us made great friends and loved every minute of it. The dreams were endless. We had one location in particular that we'd always visit. The wishing well. You can imagine the mystical spin children put on such a place. We tossed countless coins into it over the years."

"Sounds amazing." Sean remembered her talking a lot about growing up in Montana. "So why did you leave there and go to Montana?"

"My dad was military." Her tone saddened. "He relocated to Montana, and my mom's family owned a cattle ranch there. It became our home over time, but it took a while. Our last night in Alaska, the three of us were upset about the move and went to the well. With heavy hearts, we decided to make one last wish about our futures. A man with a long, white beard and rosy cheeks appeared and gave us three hand-carved coins."

"A long, white beard." Sean's eyebrows arched. "And rosy cheeks?"

"He also smelled like candy canes." Annie laughed at his expression. "You'd actually be surprised how many fit that description in North Pole, Alaska."

"What happened next?" He leaned forward, caught up in the story.

"We took the coins and each made our wish. A light burst out of the well. I can't explain it. We never could. When we turned to ask the stranger, he had disappeared. Years later, the wishes began to come true. Gabby received an antique locket that led her to her husband, Jake. Mark received an infant that needed his help, and the child reunited him with a lost love, Ally. They're married now. I don't expect you to believe it. Sometimes I still don't, but it happened, and I can't ignore that. Was it a magical coin or wishful thinking? We don't know, but I choose to believe."

"So, what did the wishing well grant for you?" Sean wasn't sure what he wanted her answer to be.

"I think my art." She got a faraway look in her

eyes. "I hit a spell where I stopped creating my paintings. I couldn't feel the inspiration anymore, so last year I took a trip here to Ireland. Things fell into place and a whole new world of ideas burst through me. I think the wish helped me find my way, and I hope it's still working on me. That remains to be seen. Whatever the case, I feel like me again. Ireland will always hold a special place in my heart."

He wanted to ask if that included him but didn't dare. "Do you believe in wishes?"

"I've asked myself that a million times, and I'll show you the answer." She stepped out of the room and returned with a large canvas. "I made these for Gabby and Mark. I have one planned for myself as well."

Sean's breath hitched as she unveiled the work. "It's amazing." He knew the word didn't do it justice. In the center, stood a large well. Three young children held out their hands as if they'd just dropped the coin. A light emanated from the depths of the well and shined upward to the night sky. At the top, slightly hidden by the light, Annie had painted Gabby with a man he assumed to be Jake. A locket hung between them.

In the bottom corners, she'd added other significant events. As Sean fell deeper into the painting, it felt real. The magic clung like a second skin. He had to step back to break the connection. He'd stared at the one in his home many times and had seen the same well, but it looked more alive, and Annie and her siblings were clear and no longer hidden in the depths. It was like the mist had parted and he could see everything just like he'd been there.

"It feels alive, Annie." Sean stared in awe and forced the waver out of his voice. "How did you create this?"

"With love. It's been in my heart for a long time." Annie stood beside him. "But I finally can paint it. I plan to give it to them for Christmas."

"They'll love it." He continued to study the painting until she walked out with a second one.

"This is Mark's." Annie turned it around.

The painting looked like the first one, except for the translucent scene at the top. He recognized her brother, Mark. The lady beside him had to be Ally. Annie had told him a little about their history. A tiny infant rested between them. The details mesmerized Sean.

"I'm not even sure what to say." He struggled to look away. "They're beyond words." He turned to Annie. "Much like their creator."

"Oh, stop it." Her cheeks flushed, but he sensed she appreciated the compliment.

"I mean it." He took her hand and pulled her close. He wanted to kiss her but didn't know how she'd react. Other than their first kiss under duress, they had avoided those entanglements.

Her eyes met his, and he lowered his head. He went slow to give her plenty of time to back away. His lips skimmed over her cheek, and he made his way toward her lips.

The loud ring of his phone caused them to jump apart. He snatched it up, glared at the name gleaming back at him, and growled. "Cara, this had better be the most important call you've ever made in your life." He listened. "I didn't forget. We're headed that way in a few minutes." He set the phone down.

"What's up?" Unfortunately, Annie had put distance back between them.

"Cara reminded me about the ugly sweater contest at the pub this afternoon. She wondered if you would be a judge. Got any ugly Christmas sweaters?" He wiggled his eyebrows.

Annie laughed. "You bet I do. Give me a sec." She put the paintings away and ran up the stairs.

Though disappointed that he'd missed his chance for a kiss, at least she hadn't run away. She'd leaned into him, and it brought hope into Sean's heart.

Annie didn't remember laughing so hard in her entire life. The sweaters she'd seen were beyond ridiculous. Her own ugly sweater didn't compare to the elaborate, hideous shirts she'd judged.

After the festivities, they served a round of drinks. Everyone toasted and stayed in high spirits.

"Sean's told me of all the places you've visited." Sean's dad, Patrick, sat beside her at the bar. "Is it all you dreamed?"

"Much more." Annie beamed. "I couldn't have imagined anything better. All the Christmas markets, a visit with Santa, Christmas caroling, and family feasts with dancing. I've tried Irish home-cooked meals and heard so many stories of old traditions and newer ones. I had to send a box of packages back home because I've bought so much. Ireland will always be a part of me. No matter how far away I am." She meant every word. Her time there had been priceless.

"Where will you be going next?" Patrick leaned toward her. "Or should I say where will you be taking my boy off to?" He winked.

Guilt washed over Annie. She'd grown to care about Sean's family, so she didn't know how to respond. She and Sean had grown closer over the past couple weeks, but neither had mentioned what would happen when the holiday ended.

"I'm not sure." She decided on a version of the truth. "I've been so wrapped up in the charming Irish traditions, we really haven't discussed what's next. I'm sure we'll figure it out after Christmas."

Patrick glanced over his shoulder and gazed at his son. His expression became more serious as he turned back to Annie. "Sean's always been a hard worker. When his mother passed, a shadow fell over him. After that, all he wanted to do was travel the world and avoid commitment. I've seen a change in him. That determined spirit has calmed within him, and he's found peace. I'm grateful to you for that, even if you do live far away." He eyed Sean again, then returned his focus to her. "Don't go telling him I said anything."

"My lips are sealed." Annie sat back and processed the information. How had this whole ruse gotten so out of hand? "And I don't think you'll ever lose him. He loves this place more than he knows—or he may not want to admit it. He's stubborn that way."

Patrick laid his hand over hers. "Oh, but there's something he loves more." He sent her a knowing look and got up from his bar stool. "If you'll excuse me, I see some friends I'd like to say hello to."

"Of course." Annie smiled at the kind man as he walked off, then pondered all he'd said as she waited for Sean to finish his shift. Part of her screamed at herself to leave and walk away. But she couldn't. She'd become trapped in her own web of deceit. She'd done the unthinkable and fallen in love with him. His dad reminded her how much Sean loved to travel, and so did she. Lately, she felt different. She'd begun to think about home and family. In those visions, she shared those dreams with Sean. She didn't know what to do or say, so she watched the clock slowly tick away.

"Hey you." She jumped when Sean came up behind her and kissed her cheek. "Are you up for a little adventure tonight?"

"That sounds ominous, especially coming from you." Annie narrowed her eyes. "It doesn't involve forty-foot jumps off cliffs, does it?"

"Not exactly." He held out has hand and had a lopsided grin. "Do you trust me? If so, I'd like to show you one of my favorite spots at the cliffs."

"I trust you." She took his hand. "But are you sure it's safe?" She tried to hide the fear in her voice. She'd never cared much for heights.

"I'm sure." He laced their fingers, and she held on tight.

The drive didn't take long, and they walked the short distance to the edge. Waves crashed below them, and the wind lifted and swirled her hair. She struggled to contain it.

The view amazed her. The moonlight cascaded down and encased them in a warm light, despite the chill in the air. It felt like they were alone at the top of the world. Two random people brought together by chance.

Sean pulled her close. "We were interrupted earlier."

"I seem to recall that." Annie tipped her head back and met his eyes. "What were we doing?"

"This." He swooped in and softly caressed her lips with his own. The touch lit a fire inside her. A passion she hadn't believed possible. Her entire world shifted. They were a perfect fit.

Tears pricked her eyes. She didn't know if he felt the same, but how could a passion so strong not be based in the truth? She held him close—afraid if she let go, he'd disappear. The kiss deepened and seemed to go on forever.

"Annie," he whispered. "What have we gotten ourselves into? I'm starting to believe in that wish of yours. It has to be a miracle that you showed up at the perfect time in my little pub. Fate brought you to me."

"I know." She leaned against him and decided to speak from the heart. "This doesn't feel like pretend anymore. It's so much more." Her deepest desires had come to fruition. Magic wish or not, she didn't care. Fate had given her a gift.

"It's not pretend." He brushed her lips and smiled. "Not for me."

"Me, either." Annie took a chance on a bigger question. "Will you escort me to my art exhibit and meet my family?"

"I thought you'd never ask." Sean wrapped his arms around her and held her tight. "I'd be honored."

His voice held raw emotion, and she finally allowed her heart to believe she'd found true love. They'd figure out all the other details. They had discovered each other, and that was enough. For now. Gabby and Mark would be thrilled and accept him just as they had Ally and Jake.

He lowered his head for another sweet kiss and her heart soared.

Sean whistled all the way home after dropping Annie off at the cottage. His life made sense, and his heart felt lighter. Annie represented everything he'd ever desired. She loved to travel and experience the world yet had a strong bond with her family. Just like him. He wondered how she'd feel about having a family of her own. She hadn't mentioned children, but based on her siblings, he imagined she didn't have an issue there.

He smacked the steering wheel with his hand.

What am I thinking?

He had them married and living some fairy-tale life. Their whole relationship began on a lie and one scorching kiss. That had changed tonight, hadn't it?

Their conversation replayed in his head. They'd talked about it not being pretend yet hadn't defined it either. He decided to head over to her house early in the morning and lay all his cards on the table. He wanted a real relationship even if it meant he had to go to some small town in Montana.

"You look bright-eyed this evening." Nana stuck her head out of the parlor. "Come have a chat with me."

She motioned for him to take a seat. "How's Annie?"

"She's good." He debated telling her the truth, but he didn't need her planning a wedding before he even asked Annie if they were that serious.

"Better than good, I'd say," Nana mocked him. "You've got that look in your eye. I may be old, but I still know a twinkle when I see it."

"I'm hopeful, but we still have a lot to work out." He stood and kissed her cheek. "And you better not interfere this time."

"Me? I'd never." She laughed and gave a pat to his cheek. "I only want what's best for you. For the last few years, you've buried yourself in work and hidden from any chance at love. I only push because you needed to break free. Take a chance."

"We'll see where it goes, Nana." Sean didn't want to give her too much hope until he knew more himself.

"Don't wait, Son," Nana cautioned. "Annie is a perfect match for you. Kindred spirits. She won't hang around forever."

"I plan to talk to her about a lot of things tomorrow. How's that?"

"Tomorrow?" She eyed him suspiciously. "Just how much do you feel for this girl? Is it that serious?"

Sean shook his head and walked to the door. "Goodnight, Nana."

"Sean!" she called as he started to turn the corner.

"Yes?" He spun to face her and tried to show patience.

"Before you leave in the morning, there's some business for us to discuss. Shouldn't take but a minute." Nana turned out the lights, then walked out into the hallway and stood beside him. "Remember, first thing."

"I'll be there." He bent and kissed her cheek again.

He climbed the steps to his room. Annie's paintings for her siblings kept popping into his mind. They were a perfect gift. He wanted to get the same type of gift for Annie, but what did you get for a creative genius? It had to be special and represent Ireland.

He called a buddy in Dublin with a few ideas. Some they discarded, but then he found the perfect gift. After an exhausting conversation of details, his plan had been put into motion. His friend promised to have it ready for Annie's big event. He'd never believed in fate until Annie walked into his pub. What were the odds?

The minute Annie walked inside, she called Gabby and Mark on a video chat to share all her news in person—or as close as she could get. They were currently at the airport waiting on their flight, and Annie gushed out every detail about Sean.

"I'm excited for you, Sis!" Gabby squealed into the phone. "It sounds so romantic."

"I agree with the *happy for you* part." Mark's gruff voice made Annie smile. "I'll have to meet him to be sure."

Annie could hardly contain her excitement. "I can't believe you'll both be here tomorrow. It seems like months since I've seen you."

"What are you going to do about traveling around the world?" Mark gave her a pointed stare. "We can't fly to every location."

"Mark, don't push," Gabby snipped. "Annie, you know he only misses you and is being ornery."

"But he has a point, and one I've thought about," Annie admitted. "While I have loved Ireland, I yearn to be back home. I miss our in-person visits and weekly meals. The two of you in my business and vice versa. I want to travel the world but maybe at a more moderated pace. I didn't understand the separation between us because you two always protected me. I know I can do it on my own, but I don't want to."

"Have you told all this to Sean?" Gabby sniffled and wiped her eyes. "He may not be ready to move to Three Forks, Montana."

Mark glared. "There's nothing wrong with our town, and it's good enough for this Sean guy."

"Of course not." Gabby rolled her eyes and swatted at him. "But his family legacy is in Ireland. What if he wants to stay in his homeland?"

"I have thought about that some," Annie admitted. "If it turns into that kind of relationship, I may have to compromise. We can split our time between the two places. I do love this cottage. The only thing missing is the two of you. Did you get the pictures I sent?"

"Yes." Gabby nodded. "And all the ones from your Irish excursions. I must admit, I'm a little jealous. They all seem like so much fun. Did you get my pics of the kiddos?"

"Yep." Annie grinned. "Absolutely beautiful. Just like their mother."

"Aww." Gabby held her hand to her heart.

"Wait a minute." Mark tilted his head. "You two are nearly identical, so I think she just complimented herself."

Gabby snickered, and Annie narrowed her eyes at him. "Well, someone had to get the looks in the family. Luckily, your kid takes after Ally."

They bickered and swapped more stories until the airport terminal announced their time to board. The attendant came over to Mark.

Annie watched as he walked away. "What's that all about?"

"Don't worry." Gabby sent her an irritated look. "You know Mark. He called a buddy and got us a special flight. He's working on some details. We better not get delayed." Mark yelled for her to hurry up. "Hold on to your britches, Bro! See you soon, Annie." Gabby disconnected.

Annie walked into the room she'd turned into a studio. All her sketches were scattered across the table. She'd packed most of her belongings but hadn't packed away her supplies yet. It had been almost impossible to choose only twelve, but that number felt right for the project. *The Twelve Traditions of an Irish Christmas.* Each scene held a piece of her heart.

She'd already painted the first one and intended to start the second. Every time she picked up the brush, her gaze strayed to the special gift she's started for Sean. She hoped what she couldn't say in words, he'd see in the painting. The urge to finish it couldn't be ignored. She switched the canvas and focused on the scene in front of her.

The colors swirled in her head as the picture took its final shape. This piece had come straight from her heart. The need to complete the images overwhelmed her. She worked for hours until the final details emerged. Her cheeks were wet from the intense emotion it evoked.

No matter what else she painted in her lifetime, she believed this one piece would be her finest. She cleaned her brushes and work area, then packed away what she could. Her thoughts returned to Sean and their time together. He'd shown her a new way to live and a new appreciation for her family.

Tomorrow, her two worlds would meet. The anticipation made her giddy like a teenager. She couldn't help it. Her alarm went off to remind her not to stay awake all night. She closed her eyes, but sleep evaded her. In the early morning hours, she finally drifted to sleep with thoughts of a bright future circling her dreams.

Chapter Five

Sean opened his tux and laid it across the bed. Excitement and anticipation flowed through his veins. His friend in Dublin had done the impossible and finished his gift for Annie. He planned to pick it up before Annie's show. Satisfied that his tux would pass Nana's scrutiny, he returned it to his closet and headed downstairs. He wanted to arrive at Annie's before her siblings, so they could talk. He had to meet with Nana first. With any luck, it would be brief. He wanted to settle things with Annie today.

He planned to profess his feelings and hoped she felt the same, so they could immediately begin a new path. He rounded the corner and stepped into Nana's office.

"Nana, you needed to see me." Sean tried to act nonchalant. He couldn't let her guess at his true feelings. She'd be planning the wedding for next week.

"Have a seat." Her eyes held a mischievous glint. Sean's stomach turned.

He took the seat opposite her. His grandfather's majestic antique desk stood between them. "I don't want to be late for Annie's."

"This won't lake long." She narrowed her eyes. "Since you're in such a rush, I'll get to the point. I know you've had your eye on the cottage for some time. It's a beautiful piece of land. Your grandfather and I lived there for a long time before we moved into the main house. Like you, we needed space."

Sean began to worry. He hoped she hadn't done something crazy with the property. Until that moment, he hadn't realized how much he wanted it. But his Nana obviously had. "What have you decided?"

"I'll give it to you on one condition." She raised an eyebrow and leaned forward. "It's yours on the day you marry Annie. I expect it won't take long for you to figure it out." She sat back with a smug, satisfied smile.

Outrage coursed through his system. "How dare you use Annie as a pawn in your warped game! She's not some toy to played around with." He launched to his feet. "I won't let you turn our relationship into a bargaining chip. It's wrong. No matter how much I love the cottage, I'd never accept those circumstances."

"Don't be absurd!" Nana's temper flared. "Annie loves that cottage almost as much as you. It's clear where the two of you are headed. Look how excited you were to see her today. This gives her a reason to stay. What does it matter if fate gives a little push to get things moving?"

An icy grip surrounded his heart, and the rational part of his brain stopped working. Annie's painting hung on the wall. Nana had always had a weakness for art and had served on the board for many galleries over the years. It was possible she knew Annie long before. What if this had been his Nana's master plan all along? That rational part of his brain tried to reason with the bigger part spiraling out of control to no avail.

His breathing became labored as facts circled in his head. Annie had shown up at the perfect time and stepped right into the role of his girlfriend. He begged her to do it. She hadn't questioned kissing a total stranger. Who does that?

"I'm an idiot." He smashed his hand down against the desk. "It was you all along."

"What are you talking about?" For the first time, Sean saw fear and concern in her eyes.

"You played your hand too early," Sean sneered. "I'm not a stupid pawn in your game. You went too far. I love you, but I'm not sure that I can forgive you for this."

Every breath sent sharp spikes into his chest. None of it had been real after all. Annie wasn't real. He fought back the emotions that threatened to break free. He refused to show any emotion there.

"Sean, stop this right now." Nana stood and walked to him. "I don't know where your mind has gone, but I had nothing to do with this. I'd never met Annie until you brought her into this house. Yes, I admired her work for years but didn't know her."

"I don't believe you." Sean hung his head. "You promised to back off."

"I kept my promise." She gripped his arm. "Don't be foolish."

"What's all this arguing?" His father confronted him. "I could hear you both out in the hall. Sean, explain yourself."

Sean gritted his teeth. "Nana set the whole thing up with Annie."

"Son, you've lost your mind. You met Annie back in the states before all of this. She came because of you."

"No, she didn't." Sean wanted to hit something but stood his ground. He'd been so blind. "I thought she'd walked into the pub one day and happened to bail me out of all the matchmaking schemes. All the while, I fell for the ultimate scheme. Well played."

Sean turned to leave the room, but his father grabbed him. "You better calm down and think before you do something stupid."

"It's not real!" Sean snapped. "Why should I care?"

"You're an idjit, Sean." His father tried to reason with him. "And even if it was some grand scheme, what's more important? Pride or Annie? You feel for the girl, and she cares for you. It's plain as the nose on your faces. Don't let her go. It'll be your biggest regret when all this anger fades."

"She was never mine to lose." Sean stormed through the door and headed to his car. He planned to confront Annie before he lost his nerve.

Cara cut him off. "What's the deal with all that back there? You don't really think Annie is involved."

"Were you in on it, too?" Sean demanded.

"You're acting like a total moran." Her Irish accent thickened. "We both met her on the same effing day. What gives?"

He shared the whole story. Instead of being sympathetic, she crossed her arms and spat on the ground. "You are an idjit and don't deserve her. Fear has grabbed you by the nether region. Nana's the excuse, but your da is right. Think about this before you go burning bridges. Maybe you can't see it, but that girl loves you."

"Why?" Sean challenged. "Maybe it's my family connections or because she's so desperate to believe in some silly childhood story. I'm done with it all."

"Sean, I'm warning ye." Cara placed a hand on his arm. "This will not end well."

"However, it ends today." Sean jerked free. "I'm never returning to this place. You can have it all. I'll stay through Christmas, then I'm outta here." The pain suffocated him.

"You're running, Sean. You need to—"

He didn't let her finish. He jumped in the car and took off, ignoring the look of pity in Cara's eyes. He intended to finish the charade once and for all.

Annie stretched her back and placed the final touches on her painting for Sean. She'd woken early and the sun had been shining for once. Her sketches laid on the kitchen table. She could already see the magic leaping from the canvas. After their time in the art gallery, she might keep them for her own display. They brought joy every time she looked at them.

Sean had promised to stop by later, and her siblings would be there any minute. Her world felt complete. A shiver of anticipation danced up her spine. Everything had fallen into place. She walked by the painting for Sean and sighed. It represented her heart. She'd give it to him tomorrow after the show. For now, she replaced the cover and moved it to the side.

A car pulled into the drive, and she peered out the window. Sean stepped out and approached the door. He seemed a little out of sorts, but she assumed his family had driven him crazy again. She'd improve his mood in no time.

"Sean, you're early." Annie opened the door and stepped back. "Come inside. Gabby and Mark will be here any minute."

"I know." His serious tone worried her. "I wanted to talk with you first."

"Okay." That feeling of uneasiness deepened. She motioned for him to sit at the table.

He shook his head to refuse the seat and avoided her eyes.

"Well, you best spit it out. What's wrong?" Dread continued to build inside her.

"How long have you known my grandmother and had this little scheme of yours cooked up?" Anger radiated around him.

"What are you talking about?" Her eyes narrowed. "I met Ava when you introduced us. I have no idea about any scheme. But you best lay it all out so we can deal with it."

"Seriously. I need to spell it out for you?" Sean scoffed. "You just happened to be at my pub at exactly the perfect time. Boom. I'm saved. Instant pretend girlfriend. All those stories about traditions, guides, and wishing wells. I should've known it was all a load of crap."

Fire erupted inside of Annie as her own temper took flight. "How dare you come here and accuse me of something so horrendous. If you wanted to call things off between us, be a man and do it honestly."

"Do you even know what honesty is?" Sean fired back. "How could you let me believe this had any hope of being real?"

"I could ask you the same thing." Annie blinked back the tears, and she crossed her arms over her chest. She kept her composure, despite wanting to break down and cry. Instead, she let the anger consume her.

"You're a jerk, Sean O'Brien," Annie grated out. "I'm not sure how I fell for all your false charm. However, I'm wide awake now. You want the truth. I'll give you all of it. I didn't know your grandmother before I met you. I helped you that day at the pub because I sensed your distress. I've always believed in helping others when I can. So, I did. My mistake. But this is one I can fix." She jutted out her chin and gave her best death glare.

"And you cared nothing about getting this cottage by marrying me?" Sean sneered. "I'm supposed to believe that."

"You've lost your freaking mind." Annie stared at him, dumbfounded. She didn't understand where all his ridiculous ideas had come from. Something must've set him off. "If I wanted a home, I'd just buy one. I already have a cabin in Montana. I'll be returning there right after my show. I'm not sure what sparked this hostility in you, but I had nothing to do with it. I'm innocent."

A moment of indecision crossed his face. "Why should I believe you? I feel like everyone is lying to me."

She touched his arm. "We may have misled a lot of people, but I never lied to you, Sean. And I won't lie now. I fell in love with you. At least, the man I thought you were. I'll get over it and rebuild my life. I thank you for proving to me that I can have those feelings. I just need to find the man who deserves them. Please leave." Her voice broke.

She walked over and opened the door.

Sean hesitated. "We should talk this out."

"I'm done talking." Annie pointed out the door. "You've been more than clear what you think of me. I guess our relationship was pretend after all. Goodbye." She refused to look at him. It hurt too much.

He tried to take her hand, and she saw regret in his eyes. They had tried to make something out of nothing and paid the price. She continued to hold herself rigid and turned from him. He eventually walked through the door.

"Sean!" Annie called out as he neared his car. "I would never have taken this cottage from you. Above all, you should've known that."

"I think I did." He bowed his head. "Can we please talk this out?"

"I'd say we're done." Annie turned back inside when another car pulled up.

Gabby and Mark got out and ran to her. She hugged them, but both siblings immediately knew something was wrong. Mark looked over his shoulder toward Sean. He took a menacing step forward. Annie grabbed him and pulled them both inside the cottage.

As soon as the door closed, Annie fell into Gabby's outstretched arms and wept until there were no tears left to cry.

Sean felt absolutely miserable. Toward the end of his argument with Annie, he had begun to realize she'd told the truth. He still didn't quite believe the pure luck of their meeting but did believe she had no involvement. In all their time together, he'd only seen her show kindness to everyone, including his family.

He'd messed up and turned his anger on her. He'd have to find a way to apologize.

He snuck up the stairs, hoping to avoid everyone. He owed a lot of apologies, especially to Nana. Despite her flaws, she always had his best interests at heart.

The cottage had sparked his inner rage. Sean had promised his mother that they'd visit the cottage soon, but he'd been busy with work when she asked. Within months, she'd gotten sick and never recovered. He always regretted not taking the time. That place had been special to them. She loved the cliffs as much as he did. The thought of anything taint-ing his home caused him to panic and act irrational. He hadn't lost his temper in years. Unfortunately, he might not be able to repair the damage this time.

"I guess it's too much to hope that you got smart-er on your way to see Annie." Cara sauntered into his room and took a good look at his face. "Nope. Stuck your foot in real deep, I see."

"Yeah, I figured it out after the fact." Sean rubbed his face, then jerked his hands through his hair. "It wasn't supposed to end this way."

"Idjit," Cara scoffed. "It wasn't supposed to end at all. Fear and grief got the better of you. Don't think I can't see why the cottage means so much to you. I loved your ma as much as my own and talked to her about many things. The guilt you're carrying is pointless. She didn't have regrets, and she wouldn't want you holding onto the past. My dear cousin it's time to let it go and embrace a new light into your life. That's Annie."

"I screwed it up." Sean closed his eyes and saw the pain that had been etched across An-nie's face when he'd brutally accused her of ly-ing to him. "I asked to talk to her more, but she ordered me away."

"And she should've." Cara glared at him. "You both needed time. The relationship between the two of you wasn't built on the right foundation. Fix it."

"I have no clue how." He met Cara's sympathetic gaze. "Would you give me a second chance after the way I behaved?"

"Not on your life." Cara snorted. "But I don't

have her kindness or gentle spirit. If you're honest with her, she might forgive you. I suggest a lot of groveling mixed with a really big gesture."

"Thanks," Sean dryly responded.

"Don't thank me." Cara shrugged. "Annie is one-in-a-million, and you let pride blind you. If she gives you a second chance, you better not mess it up. I'll side with her next time." She walked out and closed the door.

Sean sorted through all his thoughts and feelings. The tux hanging on the edge of his closet mocked him. He wanted to be there and see her in that element. To be a part of her life. Man, he'd made a mess and hurt the person he loved most. And that was the sharpest sting of all. He did love her. It didn't matter how she walked into his life. He had fallen for the beautiful artist with a heart of gold.

He picked up his phone and dialed her number. It went to voicemail. He sent a text, and it went unread. How could he apologize if she refused to acknowledge him? If only he had a time machine, he'd erase all the horrible words he'd said. He thought about driving to the cottage and demanding that she talk to him, but he had a feeling her very protective brother might kill him.

The phone rang and he dove across the bed. The screen had the name of one of his clients. He sent it to voicemail. After pacing for a bit, he called Annie a few more times and sent several text messages. The last one begged her to respond and talk to him. His phone dinged and she'd sent two words:

Too late.

His heart sank. He didn't know how to reach her. Maybe she needed time, and he had other apologies to make. He walked downstairs and squared his shoulders as he walked into the living area.

"Nana?" Sean quietly got her attention.

She simply stared at him, then nodded toward a chair. She didn't speak.

"I'm sorry." Sean reached for her hand. "I acted like a child and hurt you. I'm so sorry."

She squeezed his hand in return. "Your dad explained about your mother and the cottage. If I had known, I never would have mentioned it. My own previous actions with all the matchmaking caused your doubt in me. So, some of the blame is mine. You should know that Annie played no part in any plan. Whatever brought her to you that day, we may never know. Fate has a funny way of steering us."

"I'm beginning to understand that." Sean sighed and sat back. "I can't get through to her. What if it's too late?" Those two words Annie had sent haunted him.

"Love has its own timetable." Nana leaned over and hugged him. "But it's never too late to make things right."

He thought about those words as he sat in his room that night. He had to find the time and place to see her. She'd said she planned to leave right after the show, so he'd better come up with his grand plan soon.

A shooting star caught his eye, so he decided to make a wish.

If anyone can hear me out there, please help me find my way back into Annie's heart because she's already stolen mine. This is my Christmas Wish.

The star twinkled and disappeared.

✳ ✳ ✳

"Knock. Knock." Gabby stuck her head in Annie's doorway. "Can I come in?"

"Can I actually stop you?" Annie dryly responded.

"Nope." Gabby came over and sat on her bed. She scooted Annie over.

Annie relented and moved. "Shouldn't you and Mark be with your families? I can't believe you all flew over. It's insane to fly with that many children and a pregnant lady."

"You're our family, too." Gabby leaned her head against Annie's. "We brought them and rented a house to have a big Irish celebration for you and all of us after the show. This way we don't delay Christmas—and think of all the pictures we'll have. Jake and Ally agreed that Mark and I should spend time with you first. We missed you."

"And I missed you." Annie swiped at the tears as they escaped down her cheeks. "I'm ready to come home."

Gabby remained quiet for a moment. "That's not true, Annie. Your heart is here with Sean. Just like I didn't fight for Jake at first, you didn't fight for Sean. You know he was angry, but by the end, we could all see the pain in his expression. The regret. The Duncan triplets don't give up that easy. We each had to take the risk to see the reward."

"It's not the same," Annie whispered. "Everything was pretend. You and Mark had real relationships not a sham."

"You're being pig-headed, Sis." Mark came in and flopped on her other side. "Deep down you know it. Ally and I were brought together by an infant. We played a pretend family until we understood it was real. You're in love with Sean, and I'm thinking he feels the same."

Annie dropped her head in frustration. "How could you possibly know how I feel about him?"

"We saw the painting, Annie." Gabby placed a hand on her knee, and Mark put his arm around her shoulders. "We weren't snooping. When you tore through the house earlier, the cover came loose. I picked it up. The painting is stunning. Love radiates off the canvas. We could both feel it. From both of you. It shows a true reflection of both your hearts. I can't explain how I know it, but I do."

"Yeah, it took half an hour to stop her crying." Mark ducked when Gabby swatted at him. "Imagine my panic with two sisters weeping. You can't do that to me."

"Baby." Annie sniffled. "I did put everything into the piece. I planned to give it to him tomorrow. I guess it will go in our warehouse now. I can't bear for that to be displayed anywhere, and I can't look at it."

"Annie, you need to confront him." Gabby comforted her. "Clear the air at the very least."

"Since we're staying until Christmas, I'll find a way to speak with him." Annie smiled at Gabby's narrowed eyes. "I promise. I'll talk to him before we return. He's tried to call and text several times. He wants to talk, but I'm not ready."

"Why wait?" Mark leaned forward. "I can go get him."

"I'm sure that would go well," Annie drawled. "I can't deal with anything else. My big exhibit is tomorrow, and I'm already nervous enough. I sent in my sketch pictures of the Christmas scenes. The gallery loved them. They've already invited me back next year. I'll send the paintings, but I'm not sure I'll ever return. I have a lot to process before then. They entitled my show, *An Irish Tradition.*"

"We'll come with you. You'll never be alone." Gabby looked over at Mark, and he nodded.

"You two are the best siblings ever." Annie hugged each one.

"Better believe it." Mark pushed up from the bed's edge. "What have you got to eat? I'll throw something together."

"The appliances are tricky, but I've got some leftovers." Annie shoved them from the room. "Go warm up some food, and we'll watch a movie. We're not wasting an opportunity with the three of us alone again. I'll get back around to emotions tomorrow, but tonight is for us to feel like kids again, off on another great adventure."

"That's a marvelous plan." Gabby pulled Mark behind her. "I'll go find the perfect movie while he deals with the food. Don't be long. The Duncan triplets are going to have some fun tonight."

Annie loved the sound of Gabby and Mark bickering over the food and movie choices. It reminded her of simpler times before their Duncan triplet decree. Mark wanted an action film while Gabby would pick a comedy. They'd led a blessed life. It finally struck her that she never wanted to be a full-time traveler. She wanted someone to share the wonders of the world, but she'd always return home to those she loved more than life itself. Yes, she had a blessed life.

The smell of food drew her downstairs. She hadn't eaten all day because of the Sean fiasco. When she went into the living room, Gabby had piled blankets and pillows on the floor. Her smug expression and Mark's scowl indicated she'd won the movie battle. Annie decided not to ask and be surprised by the choice. She joined them on the floor and hit play.

The credits rolled and Annie glanced over at them. Mark had drifted off halfway through the movie. Gabby had made it to the end, but her eyes were heavy.

"Why don't we just sleep down here like when we were little?" Annie whispered.

"Sounds good to me," Gabby mumbled. "I just love that we're together. That's a miracle in itself..." She drifted off to sleep with her last words.

Once again, her sister had a valid point. Her trip to Ireland had brought her family together. That was magical.

Annie glanced at her watch and groaned. The art gallery had arranged a car service for her early in the morning. She'd have to get ready at the gallery. Gabby had agreed to come with her and help, and Mark would gather up the rest of the family coming to the show.

Despite recent events, she'd led a charmed life. She'd keep her word and contact Sean, but the outcome no longer mattered. She's found her inner peace, and someday, she'd find love. Magical wish or not.

Chapter Six

"Sean, stop being a jerk," Cara snapped and pulled him into the kitchen. "You've been rude to every customer and employee today."

"No, I haven't," Sean argued. "You're too sensitive."

"Bollocks." She poked him in the chest. "You're pining over Annie and making us all feel your pain. It's your fault, so be a man and make it right. Or suck it up and stop annoying the rest of us."

He wanted a good fight to alleviate his guilt, but it wasn't Cara's fault. "I *have* tried to call her. Multiple times. I'm certain she's turned off her phone, or she's ignoring my calls."

"You have legs. Why didn't you confront her this morning and explain how you feel?"

"Today means the world to her." Sean sighed. "It's her debut at the gallery. She's worked so hard. I didn't want to ruin everything by showing up and making a scene. I'm hoping to catch her tonight or before she leaves."

"I probably shouldn't tell you this, but since you look so pathetic and all..." Cara tilted her head to the side and sighed. "I've been texting with Annie." She held up her hand. "Shh. Not about you. Annie did happen to mention her entire family came to Ireland as a surprise. They're staying through Christmas. Her brother rented a large house not far from here. That's where Annie will be the rest of the trip. She asked me not to tell, but I believe the two of you are meant to be and equally stubborn."

"What if she genuinely doesn't want anything to do with me?" Sean flinched away from the sympathy in his cousin's eyes as he spoke.

"She doesn't strike me as a woman who would change her heart so quickly." Cara laid her hand on his shoulder. "She's hurt but don't give up on her."

Sean nodded and headed back to the bar area. He made his way around to all the patrons and apologized. He made an extra effort to show holiday spirit that he didn't feel. He'd thrown away the best thing to happen to him in years. He didn't expect her to forgive him, but he had to tell her how he felt.

His phone alarm sounded, reminding him to get dressed for Annie's exhibit. A sharp dagger pierced his chest. All the plans he'd made were useless without Annie. He slid back into his pity party and tried to survive the next hours. They had only opened for a special Christmas Eve brunch and Christmas carols. A tradition he'd hoped to share with Annie.

The door jingled and Sean froze. He didn't want to die today, but he might not have much say in the matter. The man entering the bar narrowed his eyes and walked straight toward him. He had a large canvas in one hand which didn't diminish the man's fierceness. The other formed a tight fist.

Mark Duncan.

Sean had met him a few times over the years, and of course, Annie had pictures of the three triplets set up all over the cottage. There was no mistaking him, and Annie had mentioned he could be a tad protective.

Sean took a step back and braced for the inevitable. "I know who you are." Sean tapped his own cheek. "Take your best shot. I earned it."

"I'm having a déjà vu moment," Mark muttered. "This routine is getting old. Before I crush your face, since you offered, let me ask one question. Do you love my sister?"

"Yes." Sean met his eyes. "I'm *completely* in love with her."

Mark dropped his fist. "Then, I guess I better not destroy your face. Annie might get mad at me, and she has a vicious temper when provoked."

"I noticed," Sean dryly remarked and dropped his guard a bit. "So do I at times. She wants to travel the world, and I thought I did, too. I panicked when I realized I wanted a family and a home more. Annie doesn't. It fried my brain momentarily, and I lashed out."

"Men are idiots." Mark grimaced. "My sisters are right."

Sean crossed his arms. "How so?"

"Might as well rip off the bandage and move to the groveling portion of this show." Mark spun the canvas around.

Sean gasped and fell back against the counter. He'd been amazed by all of Annie's work, but nothing compared to this. It told a love story with every brush stroke. His and Annie's story.

The moon hung high above the cliffs, casting light down onto the land beneath it. Annie had placed the two of them in the center. Their gazes were locked. They had their arms wrapped around each other in a passionate embrace. Unmistakable love beamed from their expressions. *Soul mates.* Their eyes shined bright, and the world glowed around them.

Annie had highlighted a few other places in the corners. In the top left, stood a well, faded into the background. A soft light danced from the depths. On the opposite corner, the cottage had been depicted with welcoming lights. The bottom two images made Sean's heart skip a beat. On one side, she'd painted the back gardens at his house where he'd first held her and realized he felt more for her. The final image held an Irish marketplace like the many they'd visited.

Annie had written a beautiful love story without writing a single word. He'd thrown the gift away without ever understanding. He had no clue how to fix it, but Mark might—if he was willing to help.

"What do I do?" Sean met Mark's pity-filled gaze. "I love her, and I need to tell her. Will you help me?"

"It seems to be my lot in life," Mark grumbled

and pulled something out of his coat pocket. "I'm always fixing my sisters' love lives."

He handed the envelope to Sean. "It's the ticket she had for you. I suggest you keep your promise and meet her there."

"I don't want to ruin her special night." Sean stared at the invitation and sighed.

"Do I really have to spell all this out for you?" Mark growled in exasperation. "The show will only be ruined if you aren't there. Prove you're better than she fears. Prove you'll stand up to her. And for her. That's her deepest desire. I only tell you this because I believe with everything I am that you're the one for her. If you break her heart, I'll beat you to a pulp."

With that parting line, Mark picked up the painting and briskly walked out of the pub.

Sean turned to Cara, but she pointed at the door. "Go. I've got this. Good luck."

He didn't ask twice. Instead, he rushed home and quickly dressed. The entire drive to Dublin, he worked on a plan to win Annie back.

Annie rubbed at her chest but it didn't alleviate the ache inside. She forced a smile across her face as more of the patrons gushed over all her pieces. It hurt a little more to see the first Christmas painting she'd completed on display. The scene reminded her of Sean. The gallery manager felt the piece would provide excellent promotion for next year's event. By anyone's standards, the exhibit had been a success. Yet, she felt miserable.

If Gabby and Mark hadn't come, she would've crawled into a ball and disappeared. They kept her moving and helped cover her lack of enthusiasm. Another handshake. Another smile. Her cheeks ached, and her temper began to flare. She tried to be thankful, but memories created daggers in her heart. She simply wanted to go home. To Montana.

"I need a little air," Annie whispered to Gabby. "I'm suffocating with all these people."

"I'll come with you." Gabby's concern only made it more painful.

"No." Annie gave a shaky smile. "You two cover for me. They won't know I'm missing. *Please?*"

"We can do that." Mark pulled Gabby away.

"Only a few minutes." Gabby tried to shake Mark loose. "Then, I'm coming after you."

"Promise." Annie blew her a kiss.

Annie stepped out into the cold afternoon air. She closed her eyes and tipped her head back.

Why didn't I get my Christmas wish? Gabby and Mark got everything they wanted. What did I do wrong?

The answer didn't come—only the frigid bite of the wind surrounded her. Part of her wanted to scream at the moon and demand to know why. She didn't want to end up in a psych ward, so she stayed silent.

"Hey, Annie."

She spun around and came face to face with Sean. Her heart accelerated, and she took a step back. "You shouldn't be here." She jutted out her chin and attempted to sound tough.

"You invited me." Sean moved toward her.

"That invitation was revoked." Annie pivoted again to make a move toward the door.

"Actually, you never asked me not to attend," Sean countered and reached for her arm, gently stopping her. "I'm here to support you as I promised."

"I can't do this." Annie's tears spilled down her cheeks. "Please leave and let me get through the night."

"I'd give you anything but that." Sean's soft voice warmed her heart and tripped off several alarms. "We need to talk." He released his hold on her arm.

"I'll be honest." Annie glanced where his hand had just been, yet avoided his gaze. "I can't risk my heart around you. I might not recover, and I refuse to be some old lady pining away for a love that never existed."

"But it did exist. *Does* exist." Sean tenderly took her hand. "You know it does. There's a side room right inside. Give me a few minutes. After that, if you still want me to leave, I will."

Annie fought to keep her calm. She didn't trust the hope that blossomed deep within her heart. "Gabby and Mark are waiting."

"I spoke with them before I stepped out here." Sean thwarted her escape plan. "They said to tell you that they have everything covered and to remember the decree and to follow the signs. I'm not sure what all that means, but I hope it's in my favor."

She made a promise to herself to yell at her meddling siblings later. For now, she needed a plan to get out of this conversation unscathed. Sean tightened the hold on her hand, and no matter how many times she tried to loosen his grip, she couldn't free herself from it.

"Fine." Annie followed him inside. "Five minutes. And I'm only agreeing to avoid hyperthermia."

"That excuse is as good as any." Sean went into the small room he'd mentioned.

"Well?" Annie placed her one free hand on her hip and attempted to look annoyed instead of broken. She glanced in every corner of the room except where he stood.

She forced her breathing to slow. The last thing she needed was a panic attack. Wouldn't that be a sight?

"Annie." Sean's soft voice wrapped around her. He touched her chin and guided her eyes to his, then wiped the tear that managed to escape.

"I'm so sorry." Sean held her gaze. "I'm a total idiot, and I don't deserve a second chance. But I'm asking anyway. Will you forgive me and give us another chance? A real relationship this time built on love and respect."

A million thoughts collided in her brain. Her heart wanted to say yes, but her mind didn't trust his motives. His eyes held sincerity, but they had once before. Her poor heart wasn't designed for all the drama. She needed quiet and calm.

"I forgive you for the harsh comments." Annie finally gained the courage to voice her thoughts. "I know a lot can be said when in a temper."

"Annie—"

"Wait," she interrupted him. "I need to finish this and be done. I'm not sure how, but I've fallen in love with you. That's my mistake. I don't blame you. However, I need to distance myself from you because I just can't take anymore disappointment. That's where this will end. I need to cut my losses and move on."

"If you'd stop being so pig-headed." Sean smiled when she glared. "I'm trying to tell you that I'm in love with you. Heart and soul. You big dope."

"Stop this." Her voice weakened as did her resolve against him. She didn't dare trust his revelation.

Sean reached inside his jacket pocket. Annie tried not to notice or be curious, but she couldn't keep herself from peeking. He pulled out a small jewelry box.

"I had this made a couple days ago." Sean held out the box but didn't open it. "At first, I designed it to be a reminder of everything we shared. It didn't take long for me to realize that I wanted it to mean something more. Despite the insane timeframe, I knew without any doubt that you're my one-in-a-million. My one true soul mate. We've been given a special gift."

He opened the box and Annie gasped. Inside the velvet folds lay a Claddagh ring with an amazing emerald in the center. It was encased inside white gold. The size and clarity surprised, but the implication behind it stunned her.

"Sean, what are you saying?" Her voice cracked with emotion.

"I'm saying..." He kissed her cheek. "Will you marry me, Annie Duncan, and build a real life me?"

"It's so sudden." Her mind whirled. "Is this rational? Where will we live? What would we do?"

"Does it matter?" He took her face in his hands. "Marry me, Annie."

Her heart beat out of her chest. "Yes, I will." Annie laid her hands over his. "I love you, and we'll build that life together wherever it leads."

"It's about time." He bent to kiss her before she could make a comment.

The kiss deepened, and her heart soared once again.

Sean stepped out of the way as Gabby ran in and embraced Annie. "I'm so happy for you both."

"Smart man." Mark clasped Sean's shoulder. "I knew you had it in you."

"The gallery is about to close." Annie laid her head against Sean. "What should we do?"

"I was thinking there's one more tradition that we haven't done yet. Both of our families can participate."

"What is it?" Annie crinkled her nose in confusion.

"Midnight Mass." Sean kissed her cheek. "I didn't push it before because you were set to leave, and you were preparing for this show. Despite its name, most churches offer the ceremony earlier. The one near home starts at nine. If we leave now, we can make it."

"Perfect!" Gabby bounced up and down. "We get to take part in one of the traditions. We'll do Midnight Mass tonight and everyone can come over to our house for Christmas tomorrow. Gran has been preparing food all day. We bought a few of the items, but we'd have plenty if your family joined us, Sean."

"I have a feeling my Nana would love to. She's been searching for Annie for a long time." Sean smiled. "We'll ask her tonight. She has tons of food we can bring. I can already see her delight with all those babies I've heard about under one roof. She may not ever leave. Fair warning."

"We always have room for family." Gabby leaned against Mark. "What a Christmas."

"They've definitely been exciting these past few years, and this year didn't disappoint." He pulled at Annie's hair. "What will we have to look forward to next year?" He smiled and looked at both his sisters. "I'll go pick up everyone and meet you there."

They all arrived at the church without a minute to spare and piled inside. Luckily, all the young children were mesmerized by the music and lights. The service reminded Sean of the importance of family and his mother. She would've loved Annie and her whole family. It no longer brought him grief to remember her. Instead, he felt joy.

He didn't let go of Annie's hand. Not when they announced their engagement to both families. Not when it was time to go home. He faced Annie's siblings. "I'd like to drive Annie to the cottage if you two don't mind. We still need to discuss a few things."

"Of course." Gabby hugged Annie and stepped aside.

"Actually, I'm going to spend the night there," Annie added. "The two of you should spend some time with your families tonight. Those little ones deserve the full attention from both their parents. Sean will bring me over first thing in the morning, and we'll help prepare for dinner. You've already given me all the support and love I need. As you always have and always will. I love you both."

"Aww." Gabby wiped her cheeks. "Love you, too. Are you sure you want to spend the night at the little house?"

"She has her own plans to make," Mark added as Annie nodded. "Let's leave her to it. The kiddos are exhausted."

They parted ways after a few more hugs and kisses, and Sean and Annie drove to the cottage overlooking the cliffs.

"I have a gift for you." Annie went inside, and Sean followed.

"Oh, Annie." Sean felt the blood drain from his face when she brought out the canvas. "Mark—"

"I know Mark showed the painting to you, and I understand why." Annie brought it to him. "It's still my gift to give."

He nodded and walked over to the couch. Annie removed the cover from the painting, and it still struck him speechless. The emotions radiated from the scene, depicting two people who'd come together and fallen in love. He hadn't believed in that kind of love until he met Annie. In his opinion, her creation proved the depth of their love. No other explanation existed for its beauty.

"It's the story of us, Annie." Sean took a deep breath to steady his voice. "That doesn't cover its pure beauty, but I can't think of anything stronger. This is the best gift—other than you agreeing to be my wife."

"About that." She took a seat beside him as his heart jumped into his throat.

He narrowed his eyes. "You're not changing your mind, are you?"

"Of course not, silly man." Annie leaned over and softly kissed him. "I'm concerned about our plans for *after* the wedding. We're not exactly within driving distance. Neither of us would be happy with long distance, so what's left?"

"I've thought about this a lot." Sean pulled her close and inhaled the sweet, unique smell of her. "You don't want to be separated from Gabby and Mark, and I've discovered I don't want total separation from my family, either. I suggest a compromise."

"I'm listening." Annie's smile gave him the courage to continue.

"What if we live in your cabin at Moonbeam Ranch as our main home, and make a few renovations to give a little more space? We'll keep this cottage as our second home. We'll come to Ireland every summer. My other condition is that we pick at least one place a year we've always wanted to visit, and we spend a few weeks there. It's the best of both worlds and gives us adventure."

"Are you sure?" Annie brushed his cheek. "I know you've talked a lot about traveling the world. I've come to realize it's not my dream anymore, but I don't want you to be disappointed."

"That's the thing." Sean laughed. "I didn't really want to travel. I needed adventure and excitement. Turns out you're my greatest adventure, and I can't wait to see all the Christmas traditions in Three Forks, Montana."

Annie chuckled. "You must be in love."

"They're here!" Annie called out. All of Sean's family arrived in mass. Annie suspected Nana hadn't given them much choice.

Annie and Sean had arrived early that morning to celebrate Christmas and open some gifts. The rest of the day had been spent cooking, cleaning, and setting tables.

Another knock sounded. Annie glanced at Gabby. "Who did we forget?"

"I think everyone's here unless Sean has more relatives." Gabby went to answer the door and squealed. "Mom, Dad, what are you doing here?"

"We heard about your Irish Christmas and couldn't miss it." Annie's mother kissed each of her children's cheeks. "Believe it or not, your dad insisted we were needed at Christmas this year."

Annie's dad flushed. "I had a feeling there were more announcements to be made." He patted the girls on the back and shook Mark's hand. A typical greeting from their father, yet none of them had ever doubted his love and devotion to his family. "So, introduce us to everyone."

The next hour, introductions were made, chaos with children ensued, and two new puppies peed on the floor. Finally, they all settled down to talk a little before dinner. Since both Annie and Sean had large families, they decided to skip the individual announcements that Annie's family usually shared.

Annie did tell everyone about their living arrangements and that they had decided to get married on

Valentine's Day. That brought about congratulations and one very elated Nana. Annie's dad grilled Sean a little the same as he had with Jake. Sean passed inspection. Annie's world had become complete.

"Okay everyone." Elsie got their attention. "There's one tradition I think we need to keep. Let's get dinner on the table and leave these three crazy triplets to complete their annual toast." Everyone followed her out. Ally took Nate, and Mark patted her growing belly. Jake kissed Gabby's cheek and pulled her close. Sean's Nana and aunts had taken care of the tiny triplets.

Sean brought three glasses and set them on the coffee table. "Since you're in Ireland, it's only right you toast with some Irish whiskey. I brought only the best." He squeezed Annie's hand and went back to help the others.

"I swear Gran can read minds." Annie smirked. "I have a special gift to give each of you." She went behind the tree and pulled out three canvas paintings.

"At first, I only painted two, but the third wouldn't leave me be until I brought it to life. It's incomplete, but you can see where I'm going." Annie uncovered all three.

Gabby immediately began to sniffle. "It's gorgeous and so accurate. How did you remember all these details?"

"They've been in my mind and on my heart all these years, but the past few months it wouldn't give me any peace. I had to paint them. I knew the time had come."

"Annie, I have no words." Mark's voice held so much emotion he could barely speak.

Annie stood back and studied the three paintings side by side. The wishing well in the center of all three appeared identical to the one they had thrown the coins into as children. The soft glow emanated and leapt out of the canvas. She'd depicted scenes of the three siblings and the unique journey each had taken to find love.

"Whether this whole experience happened by magic, guardians, or our triplet decree, we were each given an extraordinary gift." Annie glanced back at the paintings. "I can't even capture the true beauty of it."

"We capture that beauty every day." Gabby sighed. "Every time I look at Jake or see my children, when I see Ally and Mark with Nate, and your incredible journey with Sean. You're correct. We've been very blessed."

Mark placed his arms around each sister. "For once, I'm in total agreement. This triplet decree might be the best idea Gabby's ever had."

"Hey." Gabby jabbed him in the stomach. "I can still beat your butt if necessary."

"I have no doubt." Mark winced and rubbed his ribs.

Annie picked up one of the glasses. "To the Duncan triplet decree and whatever force brought our wishes to life. May we honor that love always and live our best life possible full of love and light."

She raised her glass as her siblings lifted theirs. "To the Duncan triplets!" all three called out.

The sound of a jingle bell captured her attention. "Did you guys hear that? I swear something jingled."

Gabby and Mark traded a knowing look. "Over by the tree." They both pointed.

Annie walked over and followed the sound. At the back of the tree, she found three ornaments shaped like coins. One belonged to Gabby and one to Mark.

"How did these get here?" Gabby eyes widened.

Mark scratched his head. "I have no idea. Mine should be at home."

"None of this has been normal." Annie reached for the third. On the back it read:

A Wish Granted For A Love That Shines

"This is insane," Gabby whispered.

Annie placed all three back on the tree. "Maybe not. We each received our Christmas wish exactly when it was meant to be. The man told us about the timeline. I wish we could thank him, whoever or whatever he is."

She turned to the tree once more to say a silent thanks for the mystery man that brought so much happiness into all of their lives.

Gabby, Mark, and Annie linked arms and went into the dining area to enjoy an Irish Christmas dinner with all their loved ones.

Epilogue

Five years later, Christmas Eve in Three Forks, Montana

Moonbeam Ranch glowed with Christmas light and cheer. Inside, everyone gathered around Gabby's infamous Christmas tree for their annual celebrations. Near the top of the oversized tree, hung three ornaments shaped like coins. Each held a special message for the three siblings and served as a reminder.

The sound of laughter filled the entire house. Children raced around, chatting and playing with their toys and cousins. The adults exchanged gifts and spoke of future plans. Gabby's latest cover designs won national awards, and their ranch had returned to a place just for family, with the exception of a few that had become like family over the years.

Gabby had a full plate with her business, three kids, and husband who adored her.

Elsie and Mick were bright-eyed as they carried around some of the children. They had been given a second chance, and it had brought new life to both of them. They traveled often and doted on their grandchildren.

Mark's new science-fiction crime series had taken off, and he'd added a new children's series and a middle grade series both full of magic and mystery. He and Ally had three children with six-year-old Nate leading the pack. Ally's vet practice had grown, and she'd added another partner to make sure she had plenty of time for family. They still lived in Mark's house and filled it with love and laughter.

Annie and Sean had traveled the world and experienced many Christmas traditions in numerous countries, but they settled in Montana and were always home for Christmas Eve. They had a beautiful set of twins. One boy. One girl. The cottage in Ireland remained their home away from home and gave plenty of time for Nana to spend with her grandbabies. Sean's painting from Annie hung above their fireplace as a constant reminder of the power of love and hope.

The three siblings stayed back to make their annual toast as everyone else made their way to the dinner table. They raised their glasses and gave thanks to that mysterious day at the wishing well in North Pole, Alaska. A breeze swept through the room, causing the ornaments to jingle. The three laughed and did another toast to the Duncan triplets. This year they added a special thanks to *Santa*.

"I do so love seeing these Duncan kids every year." The older lady stepped back and laid her head on the tall man's shoulders.

"We did well with them." He nodded in agreement. "Pure hearts since they were children. Perfect matches in adulthood."

"That's why they were chosen," she reminded him. "And they never lost that faith. Their next generation holds that same light within them."

"A promise of the future, and we'll certainly watch after them." He smiled and stepped back from the well. "Who needs our help next to find their destined wish, Mrs. Clause?"

"I know a few who could use a little nudge, Mr. Clause." She chuckled.

"So you do, and I couldn't agree more." He kissed her rosy cheeks.

Their laughter floated down into the well and flowed inside the hearts of many they'd helped over the years.

About the Author

J. L. LAWRENCE lives near Nashville, Tennessee with her family including three rambunctious teenagers. She loves reading and exploring new places. Her imagination has always provided her greatest adventures. Her daughters begged for stories that they could build together. They wanted relatable teenage angst with plenty of magic and mystery. This led J. L. to create a YA series, Path to Destiny and a new middle grade series about dragons and magic coming soon. She also has an adult fantasy adventure series, the Mystic. Please explore the website and check out her Facebook and Instagram.

authorjllawrence.com
jllawrenceauthor (Instagram)
JL Lawrence (Facebook)

Also By J.L. Lawrence

CHRISTMAS
Wishes

the antique locket

J.L. LAWRENCE

the christmas visitor

J.L. LAWRENCE

an irish tradition

J.L. LAWRENCE

J.L. LAWRENCE

Also By J.L. Lawrence

PATH TO DESTINY
SERIES

Also By J.L. Lawrence

THE MYSTIC SERIES

Made in United States
Cleveland, OH
18 November 2024